THE WITCH OF GIDEON

THE WITCH OF GIDEON

Nowhere USA Book 5

NINIE HAMMON

STERLING & STONE

Chapter One

MALACHI TACKETT PILOTED the van with the words "Healthy Pets Veterinary Clinic and Animal Hospital" emblazoned on the side down Sanders Lane in the darkness, winding away from Route 17 North into Persimmon Ridge. He turned right off Main Street onto Wiley Road for a mile or two, then left on Iron Rock Road.

The houses he passed were dark except for the one next door to Howie Witherspoon's house. Old man Hayes lived there. He was almost deaf and just about blind, and it looked like every light in the house was on. Malachi killed the headlights on the van as he pulled into the Witherspoon driveway behind Howie's car, that Malachi had parked there last night after he'd used it to take Toby Witherspoon to Sam's house.

Malachi wasn't expecting the sudden glare of the security light when he got out of the van. It was obviously hooked to a motion sensor, and he quickly darted into the shadows on the side of the garage, found his way through the dark to the side door, opened it and stepped inside. Closing the door behind him, he felt along the wall for the light switch and flipped it, filling the small, windowless building with the bilious glow from a dusty florescent light bar dangling over an old ski boat that rested on a trailer with two flat tires.

While Toby had waited in his father's car last night, Malachi had shoved the tarp-shrouded body of Toby's father under the back of the boat beneath the prop of the Evinrude engine. The dead body of Custard, the little white dog Howie had killed, lay beside it. Malachi'd figured out where to dispose of the corpses as he'd sat in the dark beside E.J.'s bed until Judd Perkins relieved him half an hour ago.

That was the best Malachi could do to delay the inevitable. Get rid of Howie's body and hide Toby. Sooner or later Malachi's mother would go looking for Howie, and when she couldn't find him and Toby, she'd suspect that Malachi was somehow responsible for their disappearance. But she wouldn't likely go after Charlie without *proof* Malachi had "lined up against her." Her favorite son could forestall her wrath for a little while, could bluff. Though playing cat and mouse with Viola Tackett was dangerous business, right now it was the only game in town.

Malachi searched the small building until he found the breaker box and turned off the juice to the outside security light. Then he hauled Howie's corpse and the body of the dog out to the van and loaded them in the back. He figured to make it to the boarded-up mine entrance just beyond the washed-out bridge on Gopher Hill Road and back to the Middle of Nowhere before dawn.

The sun was cresting the horizon out there on the flat when Malachi turned off Blandford Lane onto Lexington Road and headed down it toward the clinic. In a normal world, he'd be able to see a faint glow of light behind the mountains to the east, could watch the black velvet sky slowly turn navy blue, the color fading to pale blue, extinguishing the stars like blowing out candles on a birthday cake as light moved across the sky. Normal had taken a hike two weeks ago on J-Day. Now there was almost no transition at all between night and morning. The black didn't fade slowly away. It was black, and then it was navy and then it was blue — bam, bam and bam. Like whoever was operating the dimmer switch on the sun was in a hurry. The stars didn't blink out one by one. Stars … then no stars. They were all gone between one heartbeat and the next.

And this morning, no-stars was definitely a good thing. Malachi had noticed it on his way to Persimmon Ridge, had almost run E.J.'s van off into a ditch. All the stars were on the same side of the sky! Half the sky was empty blackness, the other half was full of stars, all the same size and as unblinking as a little kid's night light.

It was so *creepy.* When Malachi first began to notice all the weirdness-es, he thought he was the only one who saw them, that it wasn't real, just more entertaining manifestations of his PTSD. He was both relieved and horrified to discover everybody else was seeing the same things he was.

He glanced down at the fuel gauge in the van and groaned. Almost empty. It wouldn't be long now before there wasn't a gallon of gasoline to be had for any price anywhere in the county. It was a good thing he'd moved into E.J.'s apartment above the animal hospital and didn't have to travel all the way out to Killarney every night. And since his mother had stolen the Nower house in Persimmon Ridge, he'd have been stuck out there in Turkey Neck Hollow without a vehicle. Oh, he could have *taken* one — there was no shortage of abandoned vehicles in Nowhere County, the cars of the people caught outside on J-Day. But Malachi wasn't a car thief.

There was a case to be made that it wasn't stealing to take an abandoned car. That was certainly the way his mother looked at it, though she would take whatever car she wanted whether it was abandoned or not. When he'd gone to see her new "digs" last night, there had been a black Corvette parked in the driveway. He'd noticed the car a couple of times since he got back to the county after he was released from the Veterans Administration Hospital in Louisville, thought it belonged to Bud Griffith. Appeared it was Viola's now — which meant one of his brothers, probably Zach, who obsessed over cars, had taken it for his own just like his mother had taken the house.

Which was one of the reasons Malachi refused to commandeer an abandoned vehicle. It lit up the reason, anyway. When he left the county to join the military he had left behind more than Nowhere County and his family. He had made a decision the first day of boot camp, as he lay in his bunk more exhausted than he thought it was possible for a person to be and survive, that he would shed his skin like a snake and leave *everything* behind. He would no longer be Malachi Tackett in any way that mattered. He would be the polar opposite of everything his mother was, a total repudiation of the life she had created for him and his brothers and sister. From that moment on, Malachi was *brutally* honest. An inconvenient honesty that required of him that he admit to the sergeant that he'd nodded off while on guard duty, though no one had seen or reported it. The admission had earned him a week of latrine duty. And that he refused to answer for his bunkmate at roll call when Seabags missed the last bus to the base after a weekend drunk. That kind of fearless honesty had brought with it an unexpected benefit — the respect of his fellow

Marines. "Honor" was the character trait valued above all else in the Corps.

His ruthless honesty extended to what he told himself, too. He admitted his own fear in combat, never pretended things were going to work out when he knew for certain that the guano was about to connect with the air conditioning.

Like he knew right now. It was about to get reeeeally ugly in Nowhere County and there was only one way to escape the crap-storm that was about to make landfall. That was to find a road "out." The place had already been a death trap, with people vanishing without so much as a puff of smoke, their homes aging a hundred years overnight. Now, you could add into the mix the certainty that if the Jabberwock didn't get you, his mother would. Viola Tackett was a vicious murderer. She would cut down anybody in cold blood — maybe even Malachi if he got in her way. She never let an offense slide.

Somebody had to figure a way to defeat the Jabberwock. If they couldn't do that, every man, woman and child in Nowhere County was going to die. Sooner rather than later.

Chapter Two

MAYBE GRACE TIBBITS wasn't going to die after all. And that was *not* the good news. What might happen to her *instead of dying* would be waaaaaay worse.

Grace's kidneys weren't dy-*ing*, of course. They were already dead, long dead, and she'd been doing just fine, thank you very much, on dialysis twice a week in Carlisle. That's how she and her son Reece had wound up in the Middle of Nowhere on J-Day — him puking his guts out and her with the mother of all nosebleeds. Reece had been taking her to her dialysis appointment when they'd crossed the Beaufort County line, through the mirage that nobody yet knew was there, and ticked off the Jabberwock.

As soon as she stopped dialysis — "taking my kidneys to the car wash" was what she called it — toxins began to build up in her bloodstream. She and everybody else knew what that meant. It was a death sentence. Not immediate death. Unlike some people with non-functioning kidneys, hers still produced urine. So technically, they weren't totally dead. Being able to pee was a good thing all by itself, even if the kidneys weren't cleaning the blood that flowed

6

through them. People able to pee lived longer when they got off dialysis. Weeks instead of days. They still died, though, eventually. And not a clean go-to-sleep-and-not-wake-up death either. It sounded pretty grim and she'd already begun experiencing the previews of coming attractions.

She'd aged twenty years in a couple of weeks. Since she started out at seventy-five, she looked like death on a cracker — hollow-eyed, sallow skin, hair falling out. She itched all over. All over. Even under her eyelids and her fingernails. Which was impossible, of course, but tell that to her fingernails and eyelids. Her heartbeat had gone haywire — beat fast, slow and not-at-all in a perky-jerky rhythm that reminded her of the way chickens walked across a barnyard. She was swelling up like a toad from fluid retention, was exhausted by the mere thought of walking the whole twenty feet to the bathroom, though the necessity of doing that had grown steadily less — there was that, at least. She was likely confused and disoriented, too. That was one of the symptoms. But when you were confused, it was hard to tell if you were disoriented. And vice versa. The seizures, coma and death part were coming soon to a kidney-free person near her.

Or maybe not.

Might be she wouldn't be here to enjoy them. And that was way scarier than the thought of dying. Might be Elizabeth Grace Crenshaw Tibbits would just *vanish*. Go poof in a puff of smoke and be gone. But even if she *was* confused and disoriented, she still had enough on the ball to grasp that being gone from here meant being present somewhere else. Everything had to be somewhere. So where was "somewhere else"? Nobody knew the answer to that question, but best guess was the spot wasn't likely a tour bus destination.

"Audrey," she called out to her daughter. Except she didn't call out. She whispered. That was as close as she could get to calling out. "Mary Jo ... are the two of you hiding from me again?"

No, that was confusion. Her daughters weren't little girls anymore, hiding from her while their older brother Reece took the punishment for whatever it was the little imps had done. They were grown women. And Reece ... maybe her oldest son would be waiting for her when she got to wherever "not-here" was. He had already vanished.

After he blew a hole in the road, and maybe in the Jabberwock, too. Nobody'd been there to see. Liam Montgomery had called her on Saturday to tell her about it.

She can picture the deputy sheriff with his hat in his hands, worrying it back and forth between them as he speaks.

"Lonnie Monroe was the one called me. Said he heard an explosion out on the road. Dynamite. Him being a miner, he knew the sound. When he went to check it out, he found Reece's truck parked smack in the middle of the road, and there was a gigantic hole in the road, right under the Jabberwock, not fifty feet away."

He pauses.

Grace is way more than annoyed at Liam's reticence. Even before he'd been left as the lone available law enforcement officer in the county, courtesy of the imprisoning Jabberwock, he'd been hard to hold a conversation with. You had to drag the words out of him. And now she senses that his reluctance is based on the fact that he's bringing bad news. That plants a lump of fear in her belly that sharpens her tone when she speaks.

"Come on, Liam, spit it out. Where's Reece?"

"That's the part I don't know. He wasn't in his truck."

"Were the keys in it?"

"Nope, musta put them in his pocket."

"*You saying you think he just walked off? Or somebody went out there and picked him up? That doesn't make sense. Why would he need a ride if he had the keys ...?*"

Then she figures it out.

"*You think he lost a wrestling match with the Jabberwock, don't you?*"

"*That was my first thought, yes.*"

Another pause.

"*Liam Montgomery, if you don't stop fiddle-farting around and tell me where my son—*"

"*I went to the Middle of Nowhere after I got the call from Lonnie, thought maybe Reece'd be there if he'd ... rode the Jabberwock. But he wasn't there. Nobody there had seen him.*"

"*So he parked his truck, got out and blew a hole in the middle of the road.*" *She knows what that's about. He was trying to punch a hole in the Jabberwock so he could take her to dialysis.* "*And then ...?*"

"*I don't know, Mrs. Tibbits. I called his house several times and nobody answered.*"

Grace has been trying to reach Reece, too, but the phone just rings and rings. Which is crazy because even if Reece isn't home, where is the rest of his family? His wife Cissy is such a little church mouse the Jabberwock just about did the poor thing in. Apparently all she did was sit at home and cry. And she'd raised the girls, Sue Sue and Patty to be afraid of their own shadows so no way had the three of them just up and decided to go on a picnic.

"*Well ... why're you wasting time calling me when you don't even know nothing yet? Go on out to Reece's house and find him!*" *She doesn't like the fear she hears in her voice, the dread of what Liam will find when he goes looking. Or won't find.*

LIAM HAD NEVER COME to tell her what he found. She didn't even know if he'd had a chance to look before he went to Martha Whittiker's house on account of her being murdered. Maybe he'd gone to Reece's after that but she didn't think he woulda had time before the county meeting. And somebody'd shot Liam Montgomery dead at the meeting.

It didn't take a rocket scientist to figure out who'd had a motive to shoot the man, and under normal circumstances Grace would have been madder than dammit about that. Ready to lead a lynch mob out to Killarney and hang Viola Tackett from the nearest tree. Not now, though. Ever since Grace had gotten her daughter Audrey to take her out to Reece's house, she'd had bigger fish to fry than suspecting Viola Tackett'd put a hole in Liam Montgomery. Soon's Grace seen Reece's house … she'd been scared spit-less, wondering what coulda happened to him and his family.

Hadn't ever been so scared in her whole life — until *right now*.

Now, Grace was scared spit-less she was about to find out.

Chapter Three

THE BREAKFAST CLUB convened in the breakroom/war room of the animal hospital while Merrie played with the kittens and puppies and Sam's son, Rusty, spent the day with a friend.

Malachi'd had time for a shower and a shave in E.J.'s apartment after he'd dumped the bodies of Howie Witherspoon and the dog into an abandoned mine shaft. He had just settled in with a cup of coffee when Charlie arrived.

"How's E.J.?" she asked Malachi as soon as she saw him.

"Not good. I'm no doctor … but it appears to me he is getting more 'not good' every day."

"True that," Sam said from the doorway. "I just checked on him. He still has a fever, so there's an infection … somewhere. I just can't figure out where — it's not in the leg."

It would have surprised no one if an infection had developed in the gory wound where the rabid Great Pyrenees had taken a hunk out of E.J.'s calf.

"Until I can get that infection under control … he's just getting weaker and weaker."

Of course, it wasn't the injury or the infection that was most concerning. Neither was likely to kill him … but the rabies growing in E.J. daily eventually would.

If they didn't figure this thing out soon, E.J. would die a grizzly death. Bottom line, nobody in the county would survive if somebody didn't do something.

Apparently, the three of them were the only somebodies who were trying.

Well, not the only ones. There was Thelma Jackson, too, who had called the night before, telling Sam she had information she thought might be useful in their efforts to understand the Jabberwock.

As if summoned by his thoughts, Thelma appeared at the door.

"Hello, Mrs. Jackson," he said, rising. She was tall, about Malachi's height, six feet two inches, which made her slightly taller than Sam. Malachi'd always thought there was something regal about Thelma Jackson, with her wide forehead, high cheekbones and ebony skin, like she was an Ethiopian princess. She must have been a knockout when she was young because even at — must have been mid-sixties — she was still beautiful, with wide eyes and a full-lipped mouth, the kind men went all stupid over. Her hair was more salt than pepper, as glossy and shiny as he remembered it, falling in curls around her face. Her smile came easily. Soft-spoken and a good listener, she wasn't as irresistibly likable as her husband, Cotton, who'd taught math. That man could make an enemy into an ally between one bus stop and the next. But you could tell she was a true, loyal friend. The kind who'd come to get you when your car stalled in the rain at two in the morning.

"Thelma," she corrected.

"Good luck with that." Sam smiled. "I've been trying to call her by her first name for a decade and I still revert to 'she's my teacher and I can't call her Thelma!' mode eventually."

"It's nice to see you again … Thelma," Charlie said, then looked at Sam. "It *is* hard, isn't it?"

"If you don't call me Thelma I'm going to feel even older than I do right now — with the three of you grown up, pimples all gone."

They'd all been zit-faced for a time when they were in high school, but Malachi remembered Sam'd had a brush with real acne — the ghastly kind with big bumps and yellow pimples. He'd forgotten about that. Gratefully, it had left no scars, and her skin was creamy smooth now.

"Don't remind me!" Sam blushed bright red and looked away.

Malachi thought for the first time how awful it must have been for a beautiful girl to suddenly look like her face was made of ground beef. He hoped that hadn't been the reason she and her steady boyfriend, Jimbo Mattingly, had seesawed in and out of a relationship their senior year. Surely not. Malachi had barely known Jimbo, but he didn't believe a guy who'd sacrifice his life to save a child from a burning car would be that shallow.

"Have a seat," Charlie told Thelma.

"You look … tired," Sam said. "Is everything okay?"

Of course, it was Sam who noticed how drawn Thelma looked. Sam was all about other people. She'd always been like that.

"You mean, other than the fact we're all trapped here and are gradually going to be … absorbed?"

"Well, there is that," Malachi said, deadpan, and got a smile out of her.

"No, everything's definitely not okay, as a matter of

fact." She sat down heavily in the seat offered. Charlie held up her own coffee cup and nodded to the coffee pot. Thelma shook her head. "But the rest of it is …"

"Too weird to talk about?" Malachi asked, and she looked surprised, then relieved.

"We have a rule — a little like the umbrella of mercy." He didn't know if Thelma knew what that was but he didn't bother to explain. "The rule is that nothing is off the table on the weirdness scale here. Nothing in life is normal anymore, and the only hope we have of figuring this thing out is if we pool what we know. *All* of what we know. No self-editing."

"When Charlie spoke up at the meeting … I finally had somebody to tell," Thelma said. "I started thinking about this on J-Day, but … you know, we all thought it'd blow back out of here and then it wouldn't matter. And when it didn't go away, I knew there *had* to be a connection. I mean, a word like '*Jabberwock*'? — how could *that* possibly be a coincidence?"

Malachi exchanged a startled look with Charlie and Sam.

"You've heard about the 'Jabberwock' before?" he asked. "Fish just pulled the word out of his head that day. It was random. How could—?"

"Might not be as random as you think," Thelma said. "Maybe Fish heard the name somewhere before. Maybe he wasn't making it up but *repeating* it."

Sam sat back in her chair. "Goody. Another can of worms."

"I suppose we need to have a talk with Fish, too," Charlie said.

"I guess we ought to do that *before* we go to Charlie's house and try to become pen pals — no, with a blackboard, I suppose it's "chalk pals" — with the Jabberwock," Sam said.

"You're *communicating* with it?" Thelma was thunderstruck.

"It's only one-way communication so far," Malachi said. "It wants to play with Charlie." Malachi held up his hand before Thelma could launch questions. "We'll tell you the whole story, but let's take this one thing at a time. What was it you wanted to talk to us about?"

Thelma took a deep breath.

"I came here to tell you what I know, what I've found out over the years. It'll sound crazy, but ..." Her voice trailed off.

"Start small, with the history," Charlie encouraged her. "Then you can kind of ease into the Twilight Zone stuff."

Thelma nodded.

"The Jabberwock isn't anything new. It's been here for years, for centuries. Maybe all the people, the souls it absorbs ... I think it feeds on the energy. And it grows."

Her words knocked the wind out of Malachi. If that was starting *small* ... He could tell the others were as startled as he was.

"How about we back up a little." His voice sounded breathless. "How is it you know ... whatever it is you know."

"I've been tracing ancestries since I was old enough to realize that my grandmother was my mother's *mother* and that *she* had a mother, too. Like beads on a string. I was fascinated. After I retired, genealogy became a hobby. I was particularly interested in places and people who ... didn't matter."

She let that lie there in the air between them, then went on.

"That's what got me interested in Gideon. It was just a

coal camp, miners they hauled in from West Virginia and Pennsylvania — throwaway people. Nobody cared about them when they were alive and nobody noticed when they vanished."

"Then you believe Gideon actually *vanished*?" Sam asked. "Are you certain?"

"Absolutely," Thelma said. "I'm sure of it."

Chapter Four

"THELMA WAS SURE GIDEON *VANISHED*," Cotton Jackson told Jolene Rutherford and Stuart McClintock. "She was absolutely certain."

His words trailed a randomly firing synapse into the room where the three sat at Cotton's kitchen table bleary-eyed from lack of sleep.

Jolene and Stuart didn't appear impressed by that revelation, but maybe they were just too tired to show it. Coffee. And maybe some kind of pills — NoDoz or something like that. When Cotton went into Carlisle, he would stop by a grocery store and see what he could find. He didn't like the thought of getting hyped up on some drug, but they needed *something* to keep them awake — sleep deprivation did strange things to a person.

He picked up his cup and took another sip — the coffee was so strong you could stand a spoon in it.

"In the short term, a lack of adequate sleep can affect judgment, mood, ability to learn and retain information, and increases the risk of serious accidents and injury,"

Stuart said. "That last part's the kicker. It's how I won a case."

Cotton stared at him.

"How did you know I was thinking about …?"

"I could say that I just guessed. A man who hasn't gotten a decent amount of sleep since the Eisenhower Administration is staring into a cup of road tar — safe money's on he's thinking about sleep deprivation."

Stuart got up and went to the counter where the coffee pot was still gurgling its contents down into the carafe below. He picked up the unwashed cup he'd been using for the past two days, looked in it, apparently decided it didn't need washing, then poured himself a cup.

"But that's not it. I didn't guess."

Cotton felt the tiny hairs on the back of his neck stand on end.

"You gonna make *me* guess how you knew?"

"Ahhhh, snappy and short-tempered," Stuart said, while he looked around on the counter, probably searching for the sugar he'd forgotten Cotton didn't have. "Classic symptoms." He either remembered there was no sugar or gave up on it, brought the black coffee to the table and sat back down.

His face was haggard, with dark circles under bloodshot eyes. The stubble of unshaved beard and a crumpled shirt added to the effect. Cotton was sure he looked equally exhausted. But he would have to get his act together, shower and get cleaned up, before he went into Carlisle. He couldn't show up at the nursing home looking like he was homeless.

"It's like … everything's been dialed up," Stuart said. "Like my brain's an antenna and it's picking up things it never picked up before." He took a long drink of the coffee and grimaced. "Or I'm losing my mind. One or the other."

"I'm glad one of us is dialed *up*," Jolene said. She sat opposite Cotton at the table in a glorious state of bedhead. "Because my mind feels like it needs an oil change. Like it's clogged and if you drained out what's in there now it'd be so thick you could trot a mouse across it."

Cotton's head snapped up. He looked at her, started to tell her that he'd thought the same ... no, he was too tired to go there. All he said was, "I think you're picking up more than you know."

"I had a few glorious moments of clarity this morning," she said, sipping the cup of coffee she'd poured earlier that was likely cold by now. "I woke up, which would seem to indicate that I had actually been asleep, so there's that. And for a few seconds none of this was real. People vanishing, bleeding ceilings, nightmare monsters. None of it. I was waking up in my bed, hoping I wouldn't get stuck in rush hour traffic or I'd be late ..." She stopped. "And when the bubble of that glorious few moments of forgetfulness burst, reality landed on my chest with both feet. In combat boots."

She looked at them, almost pleading.

"This can't be real. I mean, come *on!* It *can't.* I want it to be over. I want normal back."

"My mama always said—" Cotton said.

"Normal's just a setting on the dryer," Stuart finished for him. When Cotton shot him a look that asked *did you just read my*—? Stuart shook his head and said, "My mother told me the same thing."

Stuart looked at Jolene over the rim of his coffee cup. "I'd settle for dryer-setting reality right now, too." Into the beat of silence that followed his words, his voice turned ragged. "But I want my wife and my little girl! I want Charlie and Merrie back!"

Then the three of them sat without speaking, each a prisoner of his own pain.

Cotton recovered first, pushed back from the table and stood.

"My mission, should I choose to accept it, is to have a long conversation with the Witch of Gideon."

"Run that all by me again," Stuart said. "I know you told me who … I'm not tracking very well."

"The Witch of Gideon is—"

"A melding of fact, fiction and folklore," Jolene interjected.

"As the story goes, the day before Gideon vanished, a little girl ran away from home and spent the night in the woods, and when she came home, the whole town was gone. So she just stayed there, in the ghost town."

"How did she survive?"

"Beats me, but apparently she did."

"Stories abound about 'witch sightings,'" Jolene said. "I mostly wrote them off because it didn't seem possible. Gideon vanished, went poof … did *something* before the turn of the century, and if there was a witch wandering around in the woods when I was a kid in the 1980s, she'd have been collecting Social Security."

"I found bits and pieces of information about that in Thelma's old files — her genealogical research — in the storage building yesterday," Cotton said, and turned toward a stack of boxes he'd set on the floor beside the back door.

Stuart waved him off.

"You don't have to show me. Give me the CliffsNotes."

"About fifteen years ago, Thelma went to Carlisle to talk to the witch's daughter, who was transferred to a nursing home there after they closed the one in Nower County. Which means that for a time there were actually two Witches of Gideon in the woods of Fearsome Hollow."

"Ahhhh, the Dread Pirate Roberts," Jolene put in and actually got a smile from the other two.

"Thelma did the math," Cotton said. "The little girl — her name was Lily Topple, by the way — was ten years old when Gideon vanished in 1895. She had a daughter, Rose, when she was twenty; that'd have been in 1905. The girl lived with her mother for a while, then I think some family raised her. I'm not sure — most of the records about Rose weren't in the shed, they were here in the house." He gestured at the emptiness. "But I remember Thelma saying at the time that Rose was seventy-five."

"Fifteen years ago, that'd make her ninety now. You really think she'll be able to tell you anything?"

"We'll see. I called yesterday and they said she could have visitors. That's what I meant earlier — after Thelma talked to Rose, she was *convinced* Gideon really did vanish overnight."

"And you want to find out from Rose Topple … what?" Jolene asked.

"Anything she can tell me about her mother, Lily — who was *there*, an eyewitness, when a place disappeared just like Nower County. There's not much information at all about her in Thelma's stored records. Maybe Rose knows something about what happened *then* that'll help us *now.* Help us … I don't know, figure out what the thing is, I guess, come up with a way to get rid of it."

"Our best chance of getting rid of it is in the equipment that *we*" — Jolene glanced at Stuart and he nodded assent — "are going back to Reece Tibbits's house to get."

"If it's still there," Cotton cautioned.

"Why wouldn't it be? What would a guy with a mouthful of bugs do with it? And when I show the readings from that equipment on my show, there'll be a whole lot more people in Nowhere County trying to figure this out than just the three of us."

Chapter Five

It wasn't until Grace Tibbits saw her breath frost in front of her that she allowed herself to believe that it really was freezing in her house and not just her imagination.

Of course, she could be imagining that her breath was frosting every time she breathed out as easily as she could imagine …

Oh, stop it.

It *was* cold in here.

She might be a confused, disoriented, dying of end-stage CKD, chronic kidney disease, but she wasn't completely crazy. Not yet, anyway, though she was surely on a fast track to getting there. It was cold in here. The temperature had been dropping for the past hour and a half.

Ever since she'd stopped calling out to Audrey and Mary Jo. If they'd heard her, they would have come. So obviously they couldn't hear her. And thinking about the why to that was worse than them not coming.

Fine. She'd do this by herself.

Most tough things she'd ever done in her life she'd

been alone when she'd done them. The going out of it, well, everybody died alone when you got right down to it. They might have had friends and family gathered around their beds, but in the actual moment of dying they were all by their lonesomes. Stepping out of life into … that was about as profoundly alone as it was possible to get.

And then you were in the presence of God, which meant you wouldn't ever be alone again for all eternity. But the moment in between, yeah, that was alone on steroids.

No different now. She was here by herself in a house getting colder and colder. Alone.

Had Reece been alone, too, at the end?

Grace had convinced her oldest daughter, Audrey, to take her out to Reece's house yesterday. Since Liam had got shot at the county meeting on Saturday, somebody needed to let Reece know his phone was on the blink, that everybody who'd tried to call had just gotten a busy signal.

She still wondered if Audrey was really so gullible that she believed that was the real reason Grace wanted to go to his house.

Probably was, come to think of it, because if she'd suspected what she was going to find when she got there she would have refused to go altogether or would at least have been prepared for what she was about to see.

They had driven down the gravel driveway toward Reece's house and Audrey had kept up a constant babble of noise, senseless talk, wondering if this was the year the cicadas would come out of the ground because if it was she was going to have to go get herself some earplugs because wasn't any way in the world to go to sleep with that buzzing in her ears.

Cicadas didn't buzz at night. Audrey knew that. And there was nowhere for her to go to get earplugs either, but

Audrey wasn't paying any more attention to what she was saying than Grace was paying to listening.

Grace glanced at the girl behind the wheel only once, saw the pinched look on her face, how she gripped the wheel in white knuckles and felt a wave of sympathy wash over her, wanted to take her little girl Audrey into her arms and tell her the mean old wasps wouldn't sting her anymore, that Reece had knocked down the wasp nest — got stung half a dozen times doing it — and had poured gasoline on it and set it on fire.

Though the woman behind the wheel clearly wasn't that same little girl, she wore the same look of fear on her face, a kind of permeating fear that only went up and down in intensity but never went away entirely.

Mary Jo had the same look.

Surely, they hadn't always looked like that. They only started when they found out their mother was going on dialysis. Or had Grace only noticed the look after she told them?

If it had, indeed, always been there, Grace was terribly, terribly sorry about that. She was their mother and if they lived in a state of constant fear, that had to be her fault somehow, didn't it? Had she just been such a strong woman, too strong after Low-Life bailed — "he died at sea," she had told the kids and they either believed it or pretended they did because they never asked about him.

She'd taken over the farm, worked it herself, only hired out the physical things she wasn't strong enough to do. She had gotten a job in town at the savings and loan and there were years of being so busy she met herself coming and going. Kids to school, her to work, pick the kids up, do the chores, fix dinner, "family time — riiiight," fall into bed to get some sleep to get up in the morning and do it all over again.

But she'd managed.

You'd think watching your mother do a thing like that would be inspiring, not intimidating. That it would make you a person of discipline and strong character. It hadn't, not with any of the four of them. Well, maybe with Oliver, the youngest, the one who went his own way. He'd always been such an independent "wild hare" she didn't know him well enough to say.

Suddenly, Audrey started screaming!

Grace was so startled she felt her own heart stop. Just stop. It hadn't been beating regularly since the toxins began to build in her system, but it had never before just stopped.

Then it commenced to flutter in irregular beats that she knew wasn't pumping no blood.

Grace began to get dizzy and a black frame formed around her vision and began to close in on her.

So she coughed. She'd read somewhere that if you were having a heart attack you should cough all the way to the hospital because the act of coughing squeezed the heart in a similar fashion to CPR. She coughed again, harder — as Audrey continued to scream. Again and again she coughed, every couple of seconds, regular-like, and finally felt her heart settle into a rhythm. About the speed of a hummingbird's heart, but that was better than useless fluttering.

Only when she'd gotten her heart beating like it should did Grace follow Audrey's gaze. She felt like screaming then, too, but she had neither the breath to scream nor the strength to do it. She heard herself make sounds, though, little sounds, whining, mewling sounds that passed for screams from the mouth of a mother who was staring at what surely was the grave of a son she didn't know had died.

Reece's house — where he lived with a wife and two daughters until a couple of days ago when he'd tried to blow a hole in the Jabberwock — was gone. Not gone as in vanished. Gone as in not what it had been before. It was ancient, looked like it was a century old. A shack. A derelict house that'd been left to rot by the owners.

The tree with a tire swing in the front had died and fallen onto the house, crushing the roof on the west end. There was no yard, no fence, no furniture, nothing to indicate anybody had lived in the house, had even been inside the house, in half a century.

Audrey just kept screaming, shaking her head and screaming. She'd run the car off the driveway into a bush when she saw the house and now she sat there in the driver's seat shrieking. Grace reached over and turned off the key, got out of the car and approached the house but didn't go inside. Couldn't bring herself to go inside. Because Reece wasn't there, of course, and because there was something so profoundly frightening about the place she couldn't have been dragged inside by a team of Clydesdales and the Budweiser beer wagon.

And the house had been cold. It was a warm summer day. The same temperature it'd been every day since J-Day. But the closer she got to the house, the colder it got. She didn't remember what happened after that. If Audrey got out of the car and got her and put her back inside, or if she had run there in terror from the cold. Her last clear memory was Audrey driving like a madwoman down the lane away from Reece's house, her eyes wild, trailing a strange keening scream behind her like the tail on a kite.

Cold.

That's what everybody said about the houses — and there were more of them every day — that had aged a century overnight. Some of them had withstood the "aging process" better than others. Some were almost unrecognizable piles of rubble. But they all had one thing in common. Cold.

So when Grace began to feel the temperature drop in her own home … well, *duh.*

As soon as Audrey helped her into her favorite chair in the living room where she could look out at the mountains through the front window, she'd begun to feel chilled. She'd dozed off then. She was always so tired, so incredibly tired, that she would fall asleep in the middle of dinner, or while she was talking. When she woke up, she'd called out to Mary Jo to bring her a blanket. Since it was clearly afternoon by now, Mary Jo had taken Audrey's place "babysitting" Mama. That's what Grace called it, though she knew in truth that she actually did need the girls' help, that her progressive weakness had robbed her of the last dignity — doing for herself. They took turns looking after her.

But Mary Jo hadn't answered.

She'd called Audrey then, louder. Well, loud for a woman who was doing well to whisper.

The house around her was silent.

And cold.

She'd called and called. They had never come and the temperature continued to drop. The view out the front window was of the mountain's shadow, hurrying across the hollow toward the house, carrying buckets of darkness to splash under the trees and the bushes, and the light would gradually fade, the sky would go from dark blue to black. The stars would come out. The wrong stars, but Grace supposed wrong stars were better than no stars at all.

She knew then.

The cold had come. Whatever that was. It was her time. And she should be grateful it was finally going to be over. Whatever it was — oh, call it by its right name, the

Jabberwock! — had taken her children and grandchildren, and Grace really didn't want to hang around without them.

It just wasn't right, though. It wasn't the way it was supposed to be. She was supposed to go first, to lie in bed with them gathered around and step out of her sick, polluted, poisoned body when it was time and into the arms of God.

But she was still here and the others were gone.

Now it was her time.

She got quiet, listened.

She could hear it coming.

Chapter Six

Cotton never could figure out why nursing homes had such foof-y names. Pleasant Acres. Bubbling Brook. Rosebud Farm. This one was Aspen Grove and as far as Cotton knew, there wasn't an aspen tree for five hundred miles in every direction. Of course, there were no Persimmon trees in Persimmon Ridge either.

Maybe the foof-names were because nursing homes were such inherently depressing places somebody'd decided that a pretty name would alleviate the drear. Putting lipstick on the pig didn't work. He wasn't a man who frequented nursing homes, shied away from them the way most people did. Who wanted to go to a warehouse for old people? At the very best, a nursing home was clean, bright and cheery with mostly well-groomed elderly people sitting in wheelchairs, staring blankly at nothing in front of them.

He'd gone with Thelma once to visit her aunt in a facility like that in Lexington. It was called The Memory Center. After the director'd waxed eloquent about all the activities they had for residents, Cotton thought they ought to change the name to Boot Camp. In the mornings, "attendants" carrying colorful signs showing the upcoming special events, greeted the residents with coffee ... to prepare them for aerobics, meditation, yoga, bowling, golf, spike the balloon volleyball, bingo, trivia — all presented with the forced cheeriness of the program director on a cruise ship.

But when her aunt's money ran out, she was moved to a Medicare facility in Richmond which was on the other end of the spectrum — dark, dreary and smelled a particular kind of bad that was endemic to such institutions. An aroma composed of, but not limited to, stale perspiration, a whiff of rancid ointment with a sulfate base, thin fumes of sour urine and the smell of illness, of being long abed and bathed only with a basin and sponge.

Aspen Grove was the second kind of nursing home. He knew as soon as he pulled into the parking lot that he was not likely to have a pleasant experience here. But he didn't know which was chicken and which was egg — did places like this attract sour, lazy, mean-spirited employees or did the presence of such people make the places what they were?

It was a one-story brick building with wings spreading out from a central hub like the spokes on a wheel. The neighborhood had probably been nice once, but now was seedy and unkempt. Unlike valued, well-tended homes that reject decay, the houses on the streets leading to the nursing home had slipped easily and gratefully into collapse, in the same way the old people warehoused in Aspen Grove would greet the prospect of painless death in their sleep.

The paint on the trim was chipped, weeds grew up through cracks in the walkways leading from the parking lot that didn't look like it had been freshly paved since Neil

Armstrong took one small step for man and one giant leap for humanity.

The place was air-conditioned, felt like it was turned up to the max … which wasn't logical since old people always seemed to feel cold. The frigid air felt like passive aggression.

The reception desk was empty when he arrived. He had to ding the bell several times before a woman emerged from a nearby office, moving with the kind of lumbering hostility of an elephant prodded against its will to stand on a ball.

"Help you?" Her name tag identified her as Hillary Clinton and Cotton wondered if it was the good news or the bad news to have the same name as the First Lady.

"My name is Cotton Jackson. I called late yesterday afternoon and asked if I could visit with Rose Topple."

She looked surprised, glanced down at a ledger in front of her on the countertop and traced down it with her eye.

"Yes, I see here that you did. You're a first."

"First what?"

"First visitor Rosie's ever had. Well, I don't know about before I got here, but nobody's ever come to see her while I've been working here and that's more than a decade."

"She doesn't have any family."

"Oh, it's not surprising for a resident to have no visitors — even the ones who do have families. They stick them here so they can forget about them. But Rosie's kinda different. To hear her tell it, she knew every man, woman and child in Nower County, but then you can't believe a word she says." She looked at him keenly. "You do know that, don't you? That Rosie's got dementia."

"Yes," he lied. "I knew that." In truth, he knew no such thing. When his wife had come to visit her fifteen years ago Thelma'd described Rose as "lucid." She'd said the woman had told such wild stories, it was possible much of what she said wasn't true, but she seemed to know where she was, who she was, who Thelma was ... and most importantly why Thelma'd come.

"You want me to tell you all 'bout my mama," Rose had said, and then she had laughed out loud — Thelma said she had "cackled." "Ever'body wants to know 'bout the Witch of Gideon."

Chapter Seven

THE ROOM GOT DARKER and darker. But Grace wasn't sure anymore that the darkness was outside her eyes. Maybe it was inside.

A sound she had been ignoring, pretending not to hear, had been growing louder and louder. It was the static sound she had heard when she and Reece had driven across the Beaufort County line and slammed into the mirage fence put up by the Jabberwock.

There were halos around the edges of her vision now, the kind you saw around lights when you drove in the rain at night. Except the halos weren't bright white light. They were black light. Light, but black. Impossible, but there wasn't anything about what was happening to her and to everybody else in the county that wasn't impossible. The light was sparkly, like someone had thrown into the air a handful of black glitter.

And it was cold. So very, very cold. Her teeth would have been chattering except she had her jaw clenched so tight in terror the muscles couldn't budge it.

This was it. This was what had happened to Reece. To

Cissy and the girls. Oh, those sweet children, how utterly terrified they must have been. This was what had happened to Abner Riley and Harry Tungate, and to all the other people out there in the county who had vanished. Nowhere County had vanished, too, and nobody out there in the wide world missed it. It could have fallen off the edge of the planet and it wouldn't even have made the ten o'clock news.

A tiny thought squiggled out of a school of thought fish below the surface and fired up into the light.

Was that it? Was that why this was happening? Was it because nobody cared about Nower County — including, no, *especially* the people who lived here? Was it possible that when the world stopped caring about a place, stopped noticing it, the place somehow ... came unhooked from the world?

Was that what caused the Jabberwock?

She heard laughter, only it wasn't real laughter. Not human laughter. It was a sound like a creature that didn't normally produce human sound was trying to laugh. Like they'd learned how by watching real people laugh at real things. It was a mimic. A parody. A mirror image of laughter. Tinny and fake and utterly repulsive.

But it was definitely somebody's ... no, some*thing's* attempt to laugh.

At what? There wasn't anything funny.

Oh, but it is humorous.

The words weren't spoken, but she could hear them. In her head. As the world around her got colder and more dim, more filled with black light and glitter. She didn't hear the words *above* the ever-increasing roar of the static, but through it.

Like whatever created the static spoke and laughed, too. Or tried to imitate speech and laughter.

No, that wasn't it. No, the laughter and the words were made out of the static. The static was the natural sound, the ambient noise, and some ... *thing* had twisted and contorted the static into sounds that approximated speech and laughter.

Approximated.

Such an ugly, hoary sound that Grace shuddered.

You don't think it's funny?

The words were a growl of ugly sound Grace suspected she wouldn't have been able to understand if they'd been spoken out loud instead of in her head.

"No." She said the word out loud and was instantly sorry she had done it. Sorry she had engaged. She didn't want to participate in any way with what was happening to her.

Let the Jabberwock kill her and eat her or dissolve her or whatever it was the thing did to people to make them vanish. Just do it. She believed a person ought to die with as much dignity as the situation allowed. The same held true for vanishing.

Chapter Eight

THE BREAKFAST CLUB sat in rapt attention as Thelma Jackson told them about digging through records in libraries all over five states — Kentucky, West Virginia, Virginia, Tennessee and Ohio — looking for information about all things Nower County, and specifically about Gideon and the people who'd lived there.

"There'd never have been a town there if it hadn't been for the coal company. Not a whole lot of people were itching to set up housekeeping in Fearsome Hollow."

"Even before Gideon, there were superstitions?" Charlie asked.

"As far back as I could find records there were mentions of the 'haints of Fearsome Hollow.' I couldn't trace where it all started, but more than just a couple of people claimed to have had encounters with them."

"What kind of encounters?"

"Not sit-down-and-have-a-cup-of-tea encounters. They were always described as terrifying. The haints were in the mist, or maybe the haints were the mist — some people said that. And it wasn't like you could build a house somewhere in the hollow and avoid the mist, since it moved around."

Malachi exchanged a look with Charlie. "We had a front-row seat at the traveling-mist show," he said. "We'll tell you all about it—"

"And about the rest of what we've figured out—" Sam put in.

"But first, we want to hear what you came here to say," Malachi said. "The people you talked to who reported haint sightings — what did they think they were?"

"Spirits of the dead. That's what a haint is, a ghost. These were particularly nasty ghosts."

"What'd they do?" Charlie asked.

"I only found a couple of incidents where anybody actually described what they *saw*. There were lots of references to hearing them, though, that they made a sound like crying children, like there was some kid hurt in the woods."

"Which would lead people out to investigate, thinking there was a lost child," Sam said and Thelma nodded.

"The descriptions I did find were remarkably similar, and they were from different parts of the hollow and separated by more than sixty years. The first one was a man named Jeb Pollock, who had built a little shack at the base of Hazard Bluff downstream from the waterfall. He was a trapper, took pelts down Troublesome Creek in the spring to the Rolling Fork, into the Licking River and the Ohio to Cincinnati."

Thelma had brought along a fat manila envelope and she opened it then and dumped the contents on the breakroom table. She searched through the pile of papers until she found the one she wanted, then she read from it. "I heared a little 'un, cryin' and went to see to it."

Thelma looked up. "What he found instead of a child

was"— she looked down again at the paper — "a beastie twenty feet tall, teeth sharp as knives, eyes like the devil, come running at me out of the mist in the trees."

"I'd heard the crying-little-kid part but not the knife-teeth part," Sam said.

"The second description was from a circuit-riding preacher named Aloushous Hardy on his way from Frogtown to Killarney who camped for the night on Buzzard Knob. He said 'The Devil his own self came to carry me away to hell. Its teeth were daggers and its eyes were full of lost souls.'"

"Correct me if you don't agree" — Malachi looked from one to the other — "but it seems like a no-brainer to me that the haints have something to do with the Jabberwock. They're both phenomena outside the range of … normal. Maybe the haints *are* the Jabberwock."

"But if the haints have always been in Fearsome Hollow," Sam said, "why'd they suddenly decide to get nasty and gobble up a town — and a hundred years later, the whole county?"

"I don't know why anybody would ever have set foot in Fearsome Hollow in the first place," Charlie said and actually shuddered. "The place is off the charts on the creepy scale and sounds like it always has been."

"Well, you have to admit that with that waterfall it's one of the most beautiful places in Nower County," Thelma said. "The coal company wouldn't have cared about how scenic the waterfall was, of course — they were just looking for a piece of flat land — but I'm sure that's why the Quakers built a settlement there."

Malachi sat up straighter in the chair and leaned toward her. He'd heard variations of the other stories she'd told — and stories about sightings of the haints that she hadn't mentioned — but he did *not* know there'd ever been another town in Fearsome Hollow besides Gideon.

"There was a Quaker settlement?"

"Yes. It was called Carthage."

"Carthage … as in the Carthage Oak." Everyone knew the huge tree in the center of Gideon was called "the Carthage Oak," but until now Malachi didn't know where the name had come from. "Did the Quakers plant it?"

"Oh, I doubt it. There's a bur oak at Airdrie Stud Farm in Woodford County that's smaller – less than hundred feet tall -- and arborists think it's almost five hundred years old. But there were mature fruit trees in the woods around Gideon that maybe the Quakers did plant. I don't know much about Carthage. I'll tell you what I do know, but first let's talk about Gideon."

Then Thelma described the coal camp built by Monroe Addington Coal, the company called simply MAC, which operated dozens of mines all over the coal fields.

"Gideon was like every other coal camp. The company slapped together some pathetic shacks and brought in miners from other coal fields in eastern Kentucky, Pennsylvania and West Virginia. And immigrants, too. The coal companies always tried to mix it up — some locals, some Irish, some Italian, some from Eastern Europe. Different languages and cultures made it less likely they would bond to their neighbors and present a united front against the companies.

"The Gideon miners who worked in the MAC #7 mine were the usual hodgepodge — West Virginians, mostly, from the Flat Top, Pocahontas, Kanawha and Greenbriar coal fields, with a handful of Irish from County Tipperary who'd dug anthracite in the Ballingarry Coal Mines. Conditions there were horrific — high up in the

Slievardagh hills, the melting snow regularly flooded the mines and drowned all the miners inside. So they packed up their families, left everything they knew behind, crossed an ocean — only to land in mines here just as bad as what they left behind."

"Even little kids worked in the mines, didn't they?" Sam asked.

"Oh my, yes. Children as young as six or seven worked alongside their parents. The smaller the better because they could get into cracks and crevices grownups couldn't, particularly mining low coal."

Malachi thought of his brief stint working in a mine, which wasn't the Hollywood version of a hole dug deep into the ground. The coal seam in eastern Kentucky wasn't in the ground beneath your feet — it was under the mountain you were standing next to. Coal mine shafts were dug straight into the base of the mountains, but since the seam was only fifty-two inches thick, the mine shafts were dug only fifty-two inches tall. At over six feet tall, Malachi had worked on his hands and knees. There weren't a whole lot of miners who could work standing up in a shaft where the roof was less than five feet off the floor. But children ...

"There was no such thing as safety regulations, working conditions were ... constant roof-falls, dangerous equipment, poison gas, explosions, breathing thick coal dust twelve hours a day. But miners were expendable, disposable, just throwaway people."

"Is that why nobody seemed to care when they all vanished?" Charlie asked.

"The person I talked to about that part said that when the miners didn't show up to board the wagons that transported them to the mine that day, the foreman did go looking for them."

"I'd think so. That's a good-sized hunk of missing

employees — they'd have shut down a whole shift," Malachi said.

"That's what I've always wondered about," Sam said. "Why didn't their disappearance raise a hue and cry? Not because anybody really gave a rip whether they lived or died but because they were indebted to the company store and you'd think the coal company would've wanted to settle up."

"What I pieced together from a couple of different sources is just an 'educated' guess. I believe the foreman was playing CYA and put out the story that the miners had packed up and left in the middle of the night, ran off on their debts and their jobs."

"But—" Sam began but Thelma held up her hand.

"I know, that story would never have held up for long. Where could they go? They had no money at all, no currency. How would they survive? All I can figure is that the Bent Stick disaster took everybody's eye off the ball."

"Bent Stick," Charlie said. "I didn't realize … the dates … yeah."

"When Bent Stick blew — all those miners, a hundred-fifty killed, more than two dozen of them children. The big city newspapers on the East Coast were all over it. Unions began to rear their ugly heads. Miners started demanding regulations and inspectors. MAC's response was just to cut bait. They shut down all their mines in this part of the state and that threw so many miners out of work nobody was of a mind to go track down a lone coal camp who'd apparently left voluntarily."

"You mentioned someone you talked to about what happened after the miners vanished — who was that?" Malachi asked.

Thelma dropped the words like stones into a still pool. "The Witch of Gideon."

Chapter Nine

JOLENE TURNED off Elkhorn Road onto the road she called Danville Pike — which apparently became Lexington Road when it came out the other side of the intersection in the Middle of Nowhere. The road signs merely identified it as County Road 278. Stuart tried to fight his way through the haze in his mind by adding up how many hours of sleep he'd lost since he'd left Chicago a lifetime ago. He gave up, decided it'd be easier to figure out how many hours of sleep he'd actually gotten — that was a smaller number.

He had slept remarkably well Friday night, all things considered, after the back-to-back gut-punch phone calls — one from the rental agency in the Lexington Airport saying Charlie had not returned the car she rented two weeks before, and the second from Charlie's publisher saying she'd missed two book-cover conference calls. But then, after all, *he could explain.* He really could explain.

So let's say Friday night — six hours, and that was generous because he'd been sipping coffee in the executive lounge at O'Hare Airport by 6 a.m. Still, call it six.

Saturday night on the lumpy cot at Cotton Jackson's house, he had likely gotten two or three hours before he woke up in the grip of the worst nightmare he'd ever experienced — the one where Charlie and Merrie were corpses …

He pushed the images out of his mind.

Say three hours on Saturday night and that was generous, too.

Last night … if he'd slept a wink, he'd been unaware of it. He'd never even gone to bed, just sat drinking coffee with Cotton at his kitchen table. He did nod off every now and then; his chin would fall forward and he'd jerk awake with a start, images of his wife and daughter filling his mind with horror.

So do the math. Six Friday, three Saturday, none last night. Nine hours of sleep between Friday night and Monday morning. That was worse than the double-dipper all-nighters he used to pull in law school.

"… ran over a striped unicorn the size of a sperm whale—"

He turned to Jolene.

"*What* did you say?"

"Ahhhh, finally. I've been sending out 'Earth to Stuart, do you read me?' messages for the past two miles."

"I'm sorry. Did you say a unicorn with purple—?"

"Just trying to get your attention. Are you with me now?"

Stuart shook his head. "Not fair — you've just missed one night of sleep. Last night was my second."

"I didn't miss the whole night. Just the part after I woke up screaming."

"You never said what the nightmare was—"

"I don't want to talk about it!"

"Ohhhh, snappy and short-tempered. Cotton was right

about the irritable part. If you had let me finish, I was going to say I didn't blame you for not wanting to share your dream. You don't have to. I've seen that film, could likely quote the dialogue."

"Nobody was talking."

"Because they were dead."

She shot him a look, but changed the subject. "Since we're discussing dead people, think we'll be seeing the Tibbits family today?"

"Reece and his charming wife and daughters — I didn't catch their names. I'm hoping they don't put in an appearance, but I think we ought to be ready for it."

"And how, exactly, does one prepare oneself to encounter a dead man with bugs dropping off his tongue and the corpse of a homicidal child?"

Jolene almost managed the right dismissive tone to hide her fear. Almost. Stuart reached down to the floorboard and picked up the tire iron he'd put there. He'd felt mildly foolish when he'd gotten it out of the trunk of his rental Lexus. But when he curled his fingers around the cold metal now, he was glad he'd brought it.

"I'm not going unarmed this time."

"You think a tire iron will stop a dead man?"

"We'll find out. I played football, not baseball, but I can put some muscle behind this thing if I have to."

"I figure we get in and out of there fast."

"Copy that. You wait in the van, keep the engine running, while I search the—"

"No way, José, you're not going in there alone."

"Okay, you unhook the equipment while I fend off the meanies."

"I've been thinking about that. It took both of us a couple of trips to haul all that stuff in there. If the various

Tibbitses try to stop us, we'll be outnumbered … with our hands full."

Stuart turned the tire iron over in his hand.

"And I'm not entirely sure it's possible to kill somebody who's already dead."

"Well, there is that."

Stuart couldn't manage a smile, but a hint of one skittered across his lips.

"All the equipment is important — I get that — but can we prioritize what we risk our lives to retrieve? Are there a couple of things that—?"

"A couple, yes. The GaussMaster EMF meter and the —" She caught his look. "Two or three of my *thingys* have the most impressive data. I'll show you which ones. In a pinch, we grab those and boogie."

As it turned out, they didn't have to boogie. Didn't have to rush at all. Nobody was home.

They could tell the difference as soon as they pulled up in front of Reece Tibbits's ramshackle house. There was no … sense of foreboding. The hairs on the back of Stuart's neck remained resolutely in place instead of snapping to attention. When they got out of the van, the air was cool, the reasonable cool temperature of an overcast day with storm clouds. It wasn't cold.

They exchanged an encouraged look, then went inside what was left of the building. They sensed no … presence. They might as well have walked into some random old building, decomposing into nothingness on the side of the road.

Stuart's head was on a swivel, surveying his surroundings, his nerves frayed, his muscles tensed. He reluctantly laid aside the tire iron he'd been clutching like a little kid's security blanket so he could help carry the equipment to the van.

He was going back in for a second load when he heard Jolene cry out. He whirled and found her fiddling with the dials on the piece of equipment she'd just set on the floor in the back of the van.

"No!" she cried. "No, no, no, no!"

She slammed her fist down on the metal casing on the whatever-it-was and turned to the smaller gizmo beside it that had several dials and knobs.

"What's wrong?"

"It's gone. It's all gone!"

She rushed past him back into the building to the large machine on the rolling equipment tray, pushed buttons, turned knobs, then let out a sigh and turned toward him. She was leaned against the equipment cart and having trouble keeping the tremor out of her voice.

"The data. It's gone."

"And that means ..."

"I set everything back to its default settings when we brought it all in here. The data, the readings we got at my father's house, it was all recorded, stored ... except it wasn't. It was all backed up ... except it wasn't that either."

He'd crossed the overgrown yard when she ran past him and he now stood in the doorway.

"So we don't have any—?"

"Proof? No, we don't. We have nothing. All my grandiose plans to lure teeming hordes of people here to see what happened ... gone."

"How could—?"

"I don't know *how* it happened, I can only tell you *what* happened. All the data has been erased."

Stuart heard himself say the words before he thought them. "Like my memories when I crossed the county line."

Her head snapped up and their eyes met. Hers were wide with shock.

"You're not saying you think it … the Jabberwock can …?"

"Maybe. I don't know."

She was silent, calculating. He watched the look on her face shift from shock through anger to resolve.

"Let's find out." She turned and picked up a machine, gesturing with her chin toward the one sitting on the floor beside it. "We'll get some *new* readings and see what happens to *them* when we take the equipment across the county line."

"New readings where?"

She paused, then looked him full in the eye. And he knew.

"At Charlie's mother's house."

Chapter Ten

SHE MUSTA HEARD WRONG.

"Me? He come to see *me?*"

"Yes, Miss Rose, there's a man who would like to visit with you." That was the ugly one Rosie called Stink Bug because she had a fat back. Who had a fat back? People were supposed to get fat in front, not down their spines, but Stink Bug looked like she'd shoved a pillow down the back of her shirt. Not that she was skinny everywhere else, of course. Mama always said that looks was skin deep but stupid went all the way to the bone. Well, Rosie'd discovered fat went all the way to the bone, too.

Stink Bug's smile looked like she'd stuck it to her face with roofing nails. She was the one who pretended she didn't notice when Rosie'd messed the bed and Rosie'd have to lie in it all night 'til the next shift of "attendants" came on in the morning and cleaned her up. 'Course the morning shift didn't like Maudie Faye for doing that no more'n Rosie did. Sometimes, Rosie entertained herself as she lay in her own crap in the dark, fantasizing all the ways she was gonna kill Maudie Faye … if she could get out of the bed, which she could, but they didn't know it. She could walk standin' straight, no hump bending her over like a broke camel. She could fly, too, like a little sparrow, one tree to the next.

Or maybe not. The flyin' part. Prob'ly not. Maybe that was part of the systems failure. She'd heard that phrase on television once and liked it, thought it had sounded more colorful than dementia or Alzheimer's — which was what they said she had, depending on which one of 'em you listened to. And she did, she knew it, watched as one batch of circuits after another in her head failed her. Names was the worst. The staff wore name tags, of course, but Rosie figured the day wasn't far off when she wouldn't be able to read 'em.

It was awful to go like that, pieces of your mind missin'. Like you left somethin' important in the attic and when you needed it, you couldn't find it.

Days of the week, months, years, who was president, things like that washed through her head and out the other side slick as eating green apples and getting the squirts. But she hadn't known any of those things when she was "wilding," neither. That was the word she used for living in the woods, making do there with her mama. She and Mama never gave a fig what day it was so she sure as Jackson didn't care now.

Some days was worse than others. The days when Rose understood that she really couldn't get out of the bed, that her legs wouldn't hold her up, days when she knew, was aware that she was shedding brain cells outta the inside of her head thick as the dandruff that rained down off the outside of Stink Bug's.

She enjoyed life more on the days she wasn't sure. Could convince herself wasn't a thing wrong with her, thank you very much, and she was pulling a monumental prank on all them idiots out there who thought there was. On days like that her mind felt too bright, like it was lit up with football stadium lights, and her 'magination took her on wild rides. Then she'd conjure up stories that she was almost sure weren't real … but maybe. Most of 'em was 'bout how she was gonna kill them as done her dirty.

She imagined pouring lighter fluid all over the orderly who was so rough when he moved her from the bed to the wheelchair that he left bruises on her arms. Chain him up and light a candle and set it next to him and watch it burn down to nothing 'til it finally lit the trail of lighter fluid. He'd watch the candle burn down, too, knowing what was going to happen to him when it did. Scared of how bad it would hurt. That's why she'd picked that fate for him, 'cause every time she saw him come into the room, she knew how bad it would hurt when he dumped her like a sack of flour into the chair.

"… listening to me?"

Stink Bug had been talking. Rosie spent so much time in her head, imagining a world that wasn't there, that she sometimes found it difficult to attend to the one that was. On-purpose dementia. Dementia she'd picked her own self 'cause it was better'n living in a reality that wasn't worth living in, hadn't been for so long she could barely even recall that time.

Rosie looked past Stink Bug to the man standing in the doorway, a big black man with a pleasant face.

Last name Jackson.

"You know Thelma Jackson, do ya?" Rosie asked him.

He looked so surprised she thought at first he didn't know who she was talking about. Then she realized he was surprised that *she* did know.

"She's my wife," he said, venturing into the room and doing a remarkably good job of pretending he didn't notice how much the room looked like some hole a creature'd dug in the ground where it dragged all its prey to kill and eat them.

"Mr. Jackson, Miss Rosie has to agree to—"

"I agree, I agree. Go on now and leave us be. I decide to die while you're gone, I'll send him to fetch you."

Cotton Jackson. A visitor. The husband of one of only a handful of other visitors Rosie had had since she was admitted to Sunny Acres, or Moonlit Fields or whatever they called the place these days. Every five years or so they changed the name.

"You gonna sit down or you gonna make me to look up at you til I get a crick in my neck and have to look at my lap for a week 'cause I can't move my head?"

He sat. The look of surprise remained on his face, so he musta expected to meet somebody 'thout the sharp edges Rose Topple had. Most people wasn't expecting what they got when they first seen her — "attendants," and orderlies and the occasional actual, no-kidding, stethoscope-wearing doctor in a white coat. She had fantasies about how she'd kill them, too, every last one of 'em, rid the earth of the bottom-feedin' carp, scavengers, white-coated monsters who thought they was God and had the power to prove it.

Doctors who could unhook machines so people would "die with dignity."

Her mama didn't want to die with dignity. She wanted to *live* — any way that presented itself. If she'd wanted to die with dignity she'd have gone off into the woods after the Vanishing and kilt herself somehow. She didn't. Just ten years old, but she clawed and scratched out a life 'thout no help from nobody. Had got pregnant after them men caught her that time, and raised up her baby girl in an unforgiving world where you had to scrape out a life best as you could, taught Rosie all about that and all the rest of it, the private stuff, the magic stuff. And then she give up Rosie for the Hendersons, who lived on the other side of Hazard Bluff in Crawford County, to raise so the little girl'd have a decent life. *That* was dignity.

In the end, Rosie'd gone home, though, to her mama. When she was a woman growed, had gone to school and worked a job and had a life … she went back to the mountains, to Fearsome Hollow. And Mama would have lived a right smart while after that if Rose'd had the sense not to trust the white-coated monsters. Mama didn't have to die at eighty-seven — shoot, Rosie was ninety now and still kicking and her mama was tougher than Rosie'd ever be. Rosie'd learned, of course, but it'd been too late to save Mama.

Rosie wouldn't need savin'. She'd step on outta this life whenever and however it suited her. But right now it didn't suit her. Right now what suited her was talking to this Cotton Jackson fella who'd come here to pick her brain about Mama. That's all anybody ever wanted to talk about and he was upfront about it, said right out that he wanted to hear about the Witch of Gideon.

Chapter Eleven

SKEETER BURKETT HAD BEEN COMING to this spot in the
Rolling Fork River to fish since he was ten years old. Him
and Buford. They hadn't been friends that first time, when
they both showed up with cane poles and plastic corks
ready to wet a hook in the same spot that summer afternoon. Skeeter was a native, Buford was from Away from
Here, his parents having moved to Nowhere County from
Beaufort County when his granny died and left them a
little piece of bottom land in Dragonroot Hollow.

Skeeter didn't take to strangers. Nobody did. And some
strange kid showing up at his spot in the river to fish was
more'n anybody'd ought to have to stand. He told Buford
if he valued his hide, he'd hightail it outta there and not
look back.

Buford asked real sarcastic-like if Skeeter owned the
river.

"I own this here piece of it."

"Says who?"

"Says me. I been fishing here every day, every summer
for the past ten summers." Which wasn't technically true

but it was close enough. "Where was you fishing last week?" Before Buford could answer, he put in, "I'll warrant wasn't here or you'd a been sitting in my lap and I recon I'd remember a thing like that."

The two of them had dropped their poles on the shore and were doing the little-kid dance, chest out, trying to look big like a rooster with its feathers ruffled. Skeeter didn't remember who shoved first. They'd been arguing that point for going on fifty years now and wouldn't neither one of them give an inch.

Buford said Skeeter shoved him. Skeeter maintained it was t'other way around.

The kids they'd been wasn't all that different from the old men they grew up to be and even now wouldn't neither one of them give an inch. After that first shove they was rolling around in the dirt, throwing wild punches that didn't land solid anywhere, rolling over and over …

Buford always told the story that it was Skeeter rolled the two of them off into the river. Skeeter, of course, knew it'd been Buford that'd done it.

And then they was friends. Just like that. They'd both done what they had to do, stood up for themselves as would make their daddies proud. They'd give as good as they'd got and wasn't neither one a winner or a loser.

So they'd climbed out of the river, sat down dripping on the bank, picked up their poles and tossed their worm-encrusted hooks into the water, like they'd been friends for years.

Skeeter found that he was smiling at the memory. When he couldn't keep his gaze from straying to the empty spot on the riverbank beside him, the smile drained off his face like water out of a pail with a hole rusted in the bottom.

Buford had been in Cincinnati visiting his daughter on

J-Day. They'd gone fishing the day before, though. Sat quiet side-by-side on the riverbank, in that way of men who'd known each other for so long wasn't no need to mess up communication with talk. Skeeter'd caught enough fish for supper, had ridden Buford hard that he was gonna go home hungry.

Now, he sat on the riverbank thinking about the exchange — "How can a man sit here all afternoon and not get a single nibble? You done lost your mojo." Mojo was a word they laughed over, one of them words the young ones used that the two old men'd snatched for themselves because it was a right handy word to use in the right circumstance.

Hadn't been but two weeks, of course, this Jabberwock thing. It could roll back out of here any time now. Any time.

It wouldn't, though. Skeeter didn't know how he knew that, but he did. That woman who'd got all up in Viola Tackett's face at that meeting said folks was vanishing and he knew that to be true, too. Folks *was* disappearing, and it'd keep happening 'til wasn't nobody left.

And would that be such a bad thing? No sense sitting out here by himself for the rest of his life. He'd rather disappear and be done with it.

He reached up and wiped tears off his cheeks — the glare off the water'd made his eyes water, that's all. He seen it then. Something had washed downriver from Ironwood Mountain and got hung up in the reeds about fifty yards upstream. A big something.

He approached it, but wouldn't let himself know what it was, even when he knew for almost certain, until he'd got right up on it and there wasn't no denying the truth of it. It was a body. A woman drowned. Wasn't no way to tell who she was, though, 'cause wasn't no face left on the front of the head. Skeeter turned his head aside and lost his break-fast soon's he seen that part. Then he took out running best as he could across the field to the neighbors, the Reynolds. Them boys was gonna have to help him get that dead woman out of the river 'cause she was fat as a boar hog.

Chapter Twelve

THE MAN GOT RIGHT to it. Rosie appreciated that. Cotton Jackson didn't pussyfoot around, didn't try to make it sound like he really was interested in Rose and not her mother. He sat down, looked her honest in the eye and wanted to know what her mama'd told her about Gideon.

"Oh, she told me everything. When I's a little girl, she told me about her whole life. Musta told me a hundred times. Five hundred. Wasn't nothing else to talk about. Told me so often that when I think about it now, it's almost like it was me and not Mama lived it."

LILY'S COUGH is better today. Some days, she hacks and hacks, makes such a racket Mama makes her go outside to keep her from waking wee Willie from his nap. Hawks up huge hunks of black goo that feel like they's ripping a hole out of her chest when they finally come loose.

Today, Rory went down with Pa. At twelve, her brother is only two years older than she is but he's a lot bigger so the foreman would rather have Lily. She can squeeze into places Rory can't, can get between the coal wagon and the shaft wall when don't look like there's enough room for a rat to get through. Won't be long 'fore Rory's so big they'll put him to work with the men and then Lily will have to go down every day. And then the cough won't never get better, breathing the coal dust in the mine for ten hours a day every day, it won't never ease up.

But she can breathe today and there's that and she ain't gonna think about later. Ma says ain't nothin' to be gained from borrowing trouble. The Good Book says every day has enough trouble of its own 'thout you going out there into the future and hauling a load of it back with you into today.

Soon's Ma takes the basket of laundry out into the backyard to hang on the line, Lily sneaks away, wants to see what happens when Mr. Milliken from MAC comes. He's the one who'll get to decide what to do, of course. Monroe Addington Coal decides everything — where you live, when you work, what you get paid — settles up your account with the company store.

Pa hadn't never been able to get square with the company, not one time since he'd brought her and Rory and Ma and the twins down from McDowell County. The company'd hired a couple dozen miners from the Flat Top fields in West Virginia, paid off what they owed and set them up with houses in Gideon, promised they could work off the debt in a year. Course, they never did. They had to eat, put clothes on their families, had to buy everything from the company store and at the end of every month what they owed was always more'n what they'd earned in wages. Even when Rory worked with Pa, and then Lily. Only one of the twins was able to work, the other one always poorly, lips blue and couldn't hardly do for herself at all. But even with little Sarah working sometimes, there was always more owed to the store than the company owed them.

When Lily rounds the corner beside the O'Leary house, she sees him, and wonders as she so often has if the devil really is a man — the mine foreman, Horace Tackett. He has an ugly, mean face with bright blue eyes that look at you like you're a smashed slug he's wiping off the edge of his shoe so's he won't track the goo into the house. He calls the Irish miners and their families "mackerel snappers." Says they should be glad of mining jobs deep down in holes under the mountains 'cause they smell so bad wasn't no other work they could do. He says every business run by decent folks had signs out front, "No Irish need apply."

Mr. Tackett always makes sure the miners know he's the biggest frog in the pond. Folks say he has bookshelves from the floor to the ceiling of one whole room in his house in Killarney, claim he has read every one of them. He likes to prance around, lording it over the miners, is always making fun of them. He calls them superstitious bobolynes — fools — because they b'lieve they's haints in the mist and are a'feared of them. He says ain't no such thing, that being scared of haints is like being scared of the "Jabberwock."

Course didn't nobody know what a Jabberwock was — that was the point of him saying it. Proving he knew things the miners didn't, was smarter than they was, better than they was. Come from some book, he said, a pretend creature in a story. Said the haints was like that, nothing but made-up monsters only stupid people believed in.

Lily knew the haints wasn't make believe. They was real. She had heard them her own self with her own ears! Lots of times. It was the horriblest thing she'd ever heard. It was always at sundown, when the mists formed above the creeks and in the trees. Her house was on the edge of town and she could hear the haints calling out to each other, crying in the nearby woods. Her mama'd always hold the little 'uns tight in her lap and rock fiercely back and forth in her rocker, hollering out Scripture and singing hymns nonstop until the sounds was gone.

Horace Tackett laughed at their fears, but he didn't laugh when Rufus Giddings come running out of the mine yesterday, hollering and carrying on about what he'd found. When folks heard, they got so up in arms about it they was near to hysterical. The miners flat-out refused to work. Mr. Tackett couldn't calm them down, so he'd called in his boss, Mr. Milliken, to talk to them.

BY THE TIME *Lily gets to the center of town, a large crowd is already congregated at the meeting place: the Carthage Oak. The gigantic gnarled tree must be almost a hundred feet tall, with limbs spread out from a trunk so huge Pa took out a tape once and measured around it, said it was nigh onto twenty feet. A big hole near the base is so large that children can play inside it.*

The man from the company is already there. Mr. Tackett stands beside two big duffel bags, the ones miners use to haul their equipment — shovels, picks, helmets, headlamps, axes and lunch buckets — into the mine.

He picks them up, one after the other, and dumps all the contents on the ground. There is a clattering sound, bones clacking against each other as they fall out onto the dirt. Big bones, little bones, jawbones, leg bones, fingers, skulls and ribs, the remains of at least a dozen people — no, more than that, two dozen. The bones aren't very big — from small people, children, too, looks like. Everybody standing near jumps back and the crowd gasps. One of the little skulls rolls like a ball toward Maggie McCarthy and she squeaks out a scream.

"See what I mean," Mr. Tackett says. "I couldn't get a man jack of 'em to lift a pick soon's we found them bones. They think the mine's haunted."

Mr. Milliken grimaces in disgust.

"How'd you come upon these bones?" he asks Rufus.

"I's diggin' at the face and knocked a hole into the back side of a cave. Wasn't very big, maybe forty, fifty feet wide and they was light shining in, around whatever was covering up the opening on the other side. Then I seen what was on the floor — bones. Skeletons of people."

Mr. Tackett describes how he got a crew of men to dig through the thick brush and move the rock away from the cave entrance and gather up the bones. But the miners still refused to go back into the mine, afraid they'd desecrated an Indian burial ground and now the ghosts of the savages would come for them in the tunnels, slit their throats or scalp them in the dark.

"This all you found, just the bones, all in that one cave?"

"Yes, sir," Rufus says.

Mr. Milliken makes a humph sound in his throat.

"Then these aren't Indian bones. The Cherokee don't bury their dead all together in caves. They bury them one at a time, dig holes in the ground so the bodies can nourish the earth. The Chickasaw put bows and arrows and pottery — all kinda stuff in the graves, things they'll need in the afterlife."

He pauses, thinking, then spits out words like they taste bad in his mouth. "These must be the bones of some of them Shakers."

He curls his mouth in a repulsed sneer, and growls, "A bunch of jitter-dancers. No-good, filthy Yankee abolitionists. They had a little town by the waterfall once 'til the Indians killed 'em off — good riddance."

He gestures at the tangled pile of bones — all that remained of a whole bunch of people. The littlest skull is the size of the apples Lily picks off the tree by the creek.

"You dragged me all the way out here for this? You might as well have found a pile of rat bones."

Lily can't pull her eyes away from the chalky white bones. The empty eye sockets seem to stare accusingly up at the crowd of people gathered around them.

Mr. Tackett speaks up then, all arrogant-like, making it clear him and Mr. Milliken are the only people present who aren't stupid.

"They're afraid of haints, scared of ghosts in the mine like they was Jabberwocks sneaking up on them in the dark."

From the look on Mr. Milliken's face, it seems for an instant that the company man doesn't know what the word Jabberwock means, and Lily feels a thrill of victory well up in her chest. But then he either remembers or bluffs.

"*No need to fear ghosts, men,*" *Mr. Milliken says sternly to the miners.* "*There's no such thing.* People *leave their spirits behind when they die, their souls, sure, destined for heaven or hell. But jitter-dancers don't leave anything behind because they aren't people. They aren't human. They have no souls!*" *He leans over and spits on the pile of bones.* "*Get rid of these and get back to work.*"

Then he stalks back to his carriage with his white handkerchief up around his nose. He always keeps it there, every time Lily has ever seen him. Ma says he thinks the miners smell like pole cats.

The arguments start then, soon's Mr. Milliken is out of earshot, standing by his carriage talking to Mr. Tackett.

"*I don't care what he says, I ain't going back in there.*"

"*We need to bury them bones, put up a cross!*" *Those words hit the crowd like a drop of water in hot grease.*

"*Wasn't you listening? It was Shakers as laid out their dead in that cave — wasn't Christians. You can't put a cross on the grave of heathens.*"

One of the Irish speaks up. "*I'll not be puttin' the likes of these in holy ground!*" *All the Irish are Catholic.*

"*We need to throw them bones away like Mr. Milliken said.*"

"*They deserve a decent burial!*"

"*Jitter-dancers don't deserve nothin'.*"

Then Oran Smalley says in his squeaky voice, "*They ain't people, but even if they was, takes more'n just one bone from a person for a proper haunting.*" *Oran is a know-it-all who couldn't pour dirt out of a shoe if the instructions was on the heel.* "*The bones from a whole body got to be all together in one spot or there ain't enough ... well, whatever it takes to make a ghost.*"

The others grab hold of the idea and run with it.

"*Yeah, all we got to do is scatter them bones out, so ain't no full skeletons. Throw them bones around in the woods, toss them all over the place.*"

A couple of miners — Pa is the loudest of them -- argue with the idea. Pa says it ain't right and proper for good Christian people to dishonor folks as had passed on like that. But they are outnumbered.

"Hey, it ain't like they was human. They was just Shakers."

Lily doesn't know what Shakers are, but whatever they are, she feels a kinship of sorts with them because Mr. Tackett and Mr. Milliken act like the miners and their families ain't human, neither.

As she turns to go back home, Mr. O'Malley calls out, "Go get yourself a gunny sack to carry 'em." He points to the small stand of thick trees that stretches from Troublesome Creek to the rocky base of Buzzard Knob. "Throw 'em in them woods, scatter 'em out."

WHILE ROSE'D reeled out the story of her mother going to the Carthage Oak that day to hear what the man from the coal company had to say, Rose had been watching Cotton, the husband of Thelma Jackson who'd come to ask her questions years ago.

She'd told Thelma all about the "Jabberwock," 'cause that was the fanciest word Rose'd ever heard and she hardly ever got a chance to use it. But she hadn't said nothing at all about the bones. Oh, no, not that part. The most important part. Rose hadn't been altogether sure she could trust Thelma, hadn't been as good as she was now at reading people.

When you sat day after day, month after month for years *waiting to die*, just watching people and not participating in conversations, after a while you learned how to read what was in people's heads and hearts even when it wasn't the same thing at all as what come out their mouths.

Rose could see through the sugar-sweet acts of them social workers who come to visit every now and then, pretending they cared what was happening to you and how you felt about it when they didn't give a fig if you dropped dead in front of them.

They phony smiles hung on they faces like them masks surgeons wore when they cut into you. She could spot phony ten miles out.

This Cotton fella, though. Wasn't nothing phony about him. Might be he wasn't telling her everything there was to tell, but she was convinced everything he did tell her was true.

Chapter Thirteen

THE WITCH OF GIDEON!

There was no way in the world Thelma Jackson had talked to the Witch of Gideon! Well ... maybe it was *possible*, but not likely. Sam had figured out the timing on Friday morning after Charlie brought in the picture of the three of them as first-graders on a field trip to the ghost town.

The old woman in the woods they'd encountered that day had said she'd been ten years old when the town vanished. That would have made her eighty-five years old when she rescued the three friends lost in the mist. And she'd be 110 years old now.

"I thought that'd get your attention!" Thelma said and smiled. "I didn't actually talk to the Witch of Gideon — whose name was Lily Topple, by the way. I talked to her daughter, Rose. It was about fifteen years ago and Rose was in a nursing home in Carlisle. She was seventy-five at the time, and her mind was still sharp."

As Sam listened, she felt a little like she was back in high school history class learning about the "shot heard 'round the world" or the Civil War or the invention of the cotton gin. Sam had developed a lifelong love of history because Mrs. Jackson — Thelma, her name was *Thelma* — had a gift for bringing stuffy facts to life. Sam remembered the day she'd held the class spellbound with the story of how the richest men in America, Andrew Carnegie, John D. Rockefeller and J.P. Morgan, had met in secret and joined their fortunes to silence the anti-trust crusade of New York Governor Teddy Roosevelt — by getting him nominated to the do-nothing job of vice president on the William McKinley ticket. "When McKinley was assassinated and Roosevelt became president … I bet it ruined their whole day," Mrs. Jackson had said.

Sam smiled at the memory

"I actually *did* talk to the Witch of Gideon, the *real* Witch of Gideon," Malachi said — which definitely got Thelma's attention. "It was a pretty harrowing experience for a little boy."

He paused then, just for a beat, and Sam knew where his mind had gone: *not as harrowing as watching somebody shoot your father dead* to keep him from killing you! Charlie was likely thinking about Toby Witherspoon, too. It was hard for Sam to pull her thoughts away from the pitiful little boy Malachi'd brought to her house last night. They'd said nothing about him to Thelma, of course. Why get her tangled up in that drama? They hadn't wanted to drag Sarah Throckmorton into it, either, but they'd had to hide Toby somewhere and the old woman who looked like Tweety Bird's grandmother was so good with children.

"And for little girls," Charlie amended, and then they told Thelma about their adventure on a first-grade field trip. Thelma listened, asked a couple of questions but mostly just listened.

"It was hard to tell sometimes if the stories Rose told me were real or just what she wished had happened,"

Thelma said. "Her mother, Lily, always came off as the hero in Rose's descriptions, sort of Tarzan meets Rambo with a side order of the Terminator. Lily was only ten years old when Gideon vanished, and she *survived*, lived off the land, all by herself. There was a smoke house where the town had stored its meat, and that didn't vanish. And she said there were fruit trees all around — which aren't indigenous to the area, but maybe the Quakers planted them. I don't think there are any there now. Berries — blackberries, blueberries and raspberry bushes. Mushrooms. There was food to be had … but still, I can't imagine how a ten-year-old did it."

"The witch — Lily Topple — told us that day that she'd run away because she got blamed when her little brother broke a pot," Charlie said.

"That's what Rose told me, too."

Thelma said the old woman had been very articulate about what'd happened to her mother, said she'd heard the stories so many times it felt like the memories were her own.

"I asked if Lily was afraid that whatever had taken all the other people would come for her, too, and Rose said no. If she had been afraid of that, she'd have left."

"Remember what she said?" Charlie said to Sam and Malachi. Then Charlie quoted the witch's words, even managed the dialect reasonably well. "It lets me and mine be 'cause we done right by it."

"*Done right by it* … I wonder what that means," Thelma said.

"Remember what else she said — that it had 'marked *us*,'" Sam said.

"And she was right about that part!" Malachi said.

Then they told Thelma what they'd figured out about why the Jabberwock had imprisoned the county — to capture the three of them. Thelma was surprised, but not disbelieving.

"Given what we know, I guess that makes sense," Thelma mused, "as much sense as any of this makes. There's a recurring theme here — little kids who run away."

"Little kids." Charlie said the words thoughtfully. "The words on my mother's blackboard — 'stay and play with me.' Almost like a little kid ..."

"The witch gave each of us a rock so we wouldn't forget her warning." Sam said and held hers up for Thelma to see. She had taken the rock out of the bowl of shells this morning, and Rusty had asked about it after they dropped Toby at Sarah Throckmorton's on Elkhorn Road.

For a moment, her son's face flashed bright in Sam's mind, and her gut yanked into a knot because he wasn't *here* where she could see and touch him. She didn't like having him out of her sight ... *people were vanishing.* But she was determined to shield him from the worst of the terror around him so she'd suggested he spend the day with his friend Douglas Taylor — just being a little boy. Dangling his toes in a creek. Playing in the woods.

Stay and *play with me.* She shook it off.

"It's a broken-off piece of a geode," Sam said and Thelma looked at it in wonder when Sam handed it to her.

"Lily *gave* the rocks to the three of you?" Thelma shook her head. "Then it must really have mattered to her that you remember. Those rocks had to be her most prized possessions. They were all she had left of her parents."

Chapter Fourteen

THE NURSE CAME to Rose's door and looked in. Stink Bug was nosey, wanted to know what Rose's only visitor in more than a decade had come to talk about.

Rose stopped talking when she saw Stink Bug there. Just looked at her.

Cotton didn't get why she'd shut up, looked from the nurse to Rose and back to the nurse.

"Is there something wrong?" he asked.

"No, I was just making sure Miss Rosie is okay. Sometimes the residents get upset or overtired when they have visitors. I want to make sure she doesn't wear herself out—"

"Horse hockey," Rose said. "You wouldn't let yore dog lift his leg and pee on me if I's on fire."

That got a rise out of her. Stink Bug's face flooded with color, but she said nothing, just turned on her heel and stalked away. When Rose looked back at Cotton Jackson, he was smiling.

She liked him for that.

"Now ... where was I?"

"You were telling me about the day your mother ran away."

Rose took up the story with what had happened to her mother when she got home from the meeting at the Carthage Oak.

LILY IS SO mad she wants to cry and throw things and kick and scream. It isn't fair.

It was Willie broke that pot. But Ma always loved him best, him being the youngest and all. And when Lily told on him he commenced to crying and carrying on, said he didn't do it. Said Lily done it and was just blaming it on him.

And Ma believed Willie! Him only four years old and Ma took his word over Lily's. She was the oldest girl, the one who took care of the twins and Willie. Ma'd believed him.

Lily had come into the kitchen and caught Willie playing with Ma's favorite bowl. She'd told Willie to put down the bowl. It was a clay pot Ma'd got from that woman who made things out of clay. It was right pretty, this one was, cause the lady'd drawed flowers and butterflies on it, painted them with bright colors. It was Ma's favorite and Willie hadn't ought to be playing with it and she told him so, told him to put it back where he got it.

Don't have to, he'd sneered and stuck out his tongue at her. She didn't get mad — at least not then. She just told him he did too have to do what she told him, and he turned to run off with the bowl, but he tripped and dropped it on the floor and it broke into nothing but sharp pieces of pottery.

Lily went after Willie, was gonna whoop his butt with a switch off a tree, but he run out the door into the backyard where Ma was hanging clothes on the line and told her Lily was trying to hurt him, that she'd broke the bowl and was trying to blame it on him.

Ma b'lieved Willie! She grabbed the broom off the porch and commenced to whopping Lily, her jumping out of the way of the blows, hollering and carrying on.

Ma chases Lily around the backyard with the broom and then Lily runs off down the trail, Ma hollering for her to come back here this minute or she'd get a whipping with Pa's belt.

Lily doesn't go back, though. She is too mad to go back, her anger like some wild horse in her chest, making her legs pump hard down the trail.

After a while she can't hear Ma yelling anymore but she keeps running, out past the men with their sacks in the woods, driven forward by anger and by a sadness and emptiness she'd never felt before.

It really was true. Ma really did love Willie more'n she loved the other five children. Certainly more'n she loved Lily. She was ten, the oldest girl. With Emma sickly all the time, Ma was always doin' for her and left Lily in charge of the others — and she told them what to do. Of course she did! But then Willie'd go crying to Ma telling her that Lily had been bossing them around, that they hadn't ought to have to do what Lily said.

How could Ma take Willie's side against her?

Just thinking the thought made her run faster. Through the trees, up the hillside with the rocks sliding out from under her feet, down into a creek and up the other side, over rocks and downed trees and through oleander bushes … On and on. She runs until the pain in her side is more than she can stand and she collapses in the dirt, heaving, sweat running down her forehead and into her eyes.

She sits there, trying to get her breath back. And it isn't until that moment that she realizes she doesn't know where she is. She has run off the trail and out into the woods … farther than she's ever gone before.

Lost.

The word is so scary she backs up from it. Scoots on her butt up against a tree and uses it to push herself back to her feet. She looks around frantically. Nothing looks familiar.

In fact, she can't even recall which direction she'd come from. She whirls around in a circle, trying to see some trace of how she'd gotten here. Nothing.

Think. What should she do?

When she spots a scuffed place in the dirt a few feet away, she knows she did it, and she races to the spot and looks beyond it for another scuff in the dirt. She finds one and she's off, running back the way she came, calling out to Ma and Pa.

She is really scared now.

ROSE PAUSED in the telling of the story, looked at the man who was listening so close he was leaning toward her out of the chair. And for the first time it occurred to her to wonder why he wanted to know the story of the Witch of Gideon after all these years. When she asked, he didn't answer right away.

"You tell me why you want to know so bad you're about to wet yourself or I ain't gonna say another word."

He looked at her, right in the eye, like he was searching for something. Like maybe if he looked hard enough he could tell whether she was as crazy as she was sure the staff had told him she was.

"I want to know because … it's happened again."

"What's happened again?"

"Gideon vanished, all the people. When your mother finally found her way home the next morning they were all gone — every single person in town. That's right, isn't it?"

"Yeah, though they's people now says that ain't true. That them people all moved away or went somewhere 'thout telling anybody. One fella told Ma when she was in her twenties that she'd made it all up, that her family had moved away and left her behind because she was so ugly."

He was one of them. The four men who caught Ma.

They'd a'kept her and used her 'til they killed her if she hadn't cut the leader, cut him bad and then run.

"Your mother's story is true. Every word of it. I know that because other people have vanished, the same way."

Rose was so surprised she just looked at him.

"In fact … everybody in Nower County. They're all gone. I came home from work in Lexington and the whole county was empty."

"You're making that up! Ain't no way that's true. If it was, I'd a'heard about it. They's news shows on the television in the craft room, stuff on there about wars and the like … that building in Oklahoma City that was blowed up last month. If Nower County — the whole place disappeared … It'd a been on the news."

"Nobody believed me."

That stopped her cold. Not just that he said it, but *the way* he said it, with the same mixture of emotions that'd been in her mother's voice when she'd described telling Mr. Tackett when he come to pick up the miners for their shift — *they's gone, everybody's gone!* Terror and anger and confusion and outrage and … all tangled up together.

"You told …?"

"The state police, the sheriff's departments in every surrounding county. I even went to the FBI."

"And wouldn't none of those people go see for theirselves?"

"They all did. And they saw what I told them they'd see — that everybody was gone. They saw that every word I'd told them was true."

"Then what …?"

"As soon as they crossed the Nower County line to leave … they forgot what they'd seen."

That set Rose's mind spinning and that wasn't a good

thing since the machinery in her head wasn't in very good repair.

"When did they … how long ago?"

"Two weeks."

"Some of them people's still there, then. Maybe not all of 'em, but some."

"Still there?" Cotton's voice was tight.

"Like my family and all them other folks was still there in Gideon … for a little while. Mama's daddy was still there for three days. She knew 'cause he left rocks for her to find."

Tears stream down Lily's face when she figures it out. Her father left her the rocks to tell her he was still there, still alive, a message. But there is no rock today. Wasn't one yesterday or the day before. He'd left three pieces of that geode, but not the fourth piece. An empty trail sends its own message. Her father … her mother and brothers and sisters … all the people in Gideon — they're really not there anymore. They are gone.

Cotton sat quiet after Rose told him the story. She knew that had to be hard to put it all together in his head. She hadn't never had to try. It was just the world she lived in.

"My friend Stuart saw someone through the mirage on the road, on the other side, but he vanished and Stuart never had a chance to talk to him."

"Your friend seen the Jabberwock gobble that man up, watched it happen?" She could hear the awe in her own words.

"Jabberwock?" He looked surprised. "Your mother named it that, the Jabberwock, because of what Mr. Tackett said?"

"No, the Jabberwock took the name its own self."

"How do you know that?"

"The Jabberwock told Mama."

Cotton's eyes turned sharp but there was no disbelief in them. "She talked to it?"

Rose nodded. "He told her things."

"What things?"

"Just … things. Mama and the Jabberwock, they had things to say to each other after Mama done what she done."

"What did she do?"

Rose realized she'd gone too far, said too much, so she stopped talking. Wanted the man named Cotton to go away because she was tired and her mind had got that fuzzy feeling, so she couldn't tell if what she said was true. Like being able to fly. Like that. Might be what she'd already said wasn't true.

It was just that she didn't never have anybody to talk to about anything, let alone the most important thing of all.

"She done right by the Jabberwock, that's all. That's why it left her be. I ain't gonna say no more."

And she didn't.

Chapter Fifteen

WHAT THELMA DESCRIBED to them about the rocks Lily Topple found on the trail matched up like perfect puzzle pieces to what the old woman had told Charlie and Sam and Malachi.

"When we first started comparing Gideon Witch stories a couple of days ago, Sam mentioned how Liam had tossed a rock through the Jabberwock that first day to see if it'd vanish," Charlie said. "Do you think maybe Lily's father could see through the Jabberwock like that, maybe even see the little girl standing there on the trail?"

"I don't believe the Jabberwock is the same now as it was a hundred years ago. It's much bigger and stronger. That'd be the natural progression, don't you think?"

"And you say Rose Topple called it 'the Jabberwock'?" Sam said. "Did she tell you why?"

"She said her mother called it that because that's what it was. She said" — Thelma paused to get it right — "'it didn't have no name so it took the Jabberwock for its very own.'"

"How would her mother have known that unless …?" Charlie asked.

"The Jabberwock told her. It talked to her." Thelma held up a hand to ward off the host of questions she could see coming. "I asked about it and Rose wouldn't say any more. Which, of course, begs a whole host of other questions — how did it talk to her? What form did the communication take? It wasn't words on a blackboard. Even if there'd been one, Lily Topple couldn't read."

Charlie shook her head. Her voice was soft. "And what *else* did the Jabberwock tell Lily that it'd be reeeeally helpful to know right now?"

The group was quiet for a little while, each lost in their own thoughts. Then Malachi picked up the conversational ball and ran a different way with it.

"You said you'd get back to it later," Malachi said. "I want to hear about the Quaker village that was there before Gideon."

Charlie stopped breathing. She had been dreading this part.

"Did it … *vanish*, too?" she asked.

"It disappeared, but it didn't vanish. It was wiped out by Indians and burned to the ground."

"Well, *that's* good news!" Charlie said, then looked around. "I don't mean good news that all those people were massacred, but—"

"We get it," Malachi said.

"There's not much of a story to tell. Quakers were part of the westward migration through the Cumberland Gap after Thomas Walker discovered it in 1750, and apparently, a small group of them crossed the mountains and decided to stay in Fearsome Hollow, built a settlement they called Carthage by the waterfall."

"Why?" Sam asked. "I mean, it's a beautiful place and

all, but why would you settle in mountains? The Quakers were farmers, weren't they? Not a whole lot of tillable land in Fearsome Hollow."

"Not now, there isn't, but we're talking almost two hundred years ago. Topography changes. It wasn't a very big village, I don't think, a handful of families with lots of kids, maybe — so there must have been enough land to grow crops to feed themselves. And remember, the woods were teeming with game. Boonesborough had been there for twenty years by 1795 and it would have been a thriving little metropolis — less than a week's travel away."

"Sure … just a week on horseback, right next door," Malachi said.

"Maybe they settled in Fearsome Hollow *because* it was remote. The people in Boonesborough might really have been the nearest neighbors."

"Which meant nobody saw the smoke and came running to help," Charlie said.

"They might not have come running even if they'd seen smoke. The Quakers weren't popular among the other settlers who branched out from Virginia. They dressed funny, held to strict moral codes about honorable behavior and honesty."

"And that made them people you definitely wanted to avoid because …?" Sam asked.

"They had other queer ideas — you know, like God created all people equal — the radical ideology that prompted Pennsylvania Quakers to build the Underground Railroad."

Thelma smiled.

"They didn't *lie* when they told authorities there were no slaves on the premises — because in their minds, the people with black skin hiding in their root cellars were *not* slaves."

"Quakers were pacifists, weren't they?" Sam asked and Thelma nodded.

"And that would have been problematic. On the frontier, settlers had to band together to protect themselves against the Indians. The Quakers wouldn't fight — which, I'm sure, is why the village was wiped out when the Indians attacked."

"If the people were massacred, and the village burned down, and there weren't any neighbors ... how did you find out they were there in the first place, or what happened to them?" Malachi asked.

"I was looking up the genealogy records of the Tibbits family — traced them back to Boonesborough. Vernon Tibbits ran an inn there — but more important, his wife Naomi faithfully kept a diary!"

Charlie smiled, imagining Thelma's face when she came upon such a treasure trove of historical information.

"An entry dated 18 June, 1820 mentioned a woman who stayed at the inn whose name was Mary Whitt."

Thelma reached out to the pile of information she'd dumped on the table from the manila envelope and pulled from it a notebook. She flipped through the pages until she found what she was looking for.

"Naomi wrote that Mary Whitt was a white woman who'd been held captive by Indians for twenty-five years." Thelma read from the page, "Mary was a Quaker and they built a town called Carthage beside the waterfall on Troublesome Creek. Then the Indians come, kilt the men, carried off the women, and burned everything to the ground. So the Indian raid must have been in 1795."

"That's all you know about Carthage?" Malachi asked.

"No. Have you ever been to Shakertown?"

Malachi and Sam shook their heads but Charlie said, "I have."

"When I was in college a group of us went down to Pleasant Hill to eat in the restaurant." They'd toured the grounds, too, explored dozens of preserved buildings that displayed the Shakers' amazing craftsmanship. "I didn't know that Shakers and Quakers were the same thing."

"Oh, they're not, but they're similar." That sent Thelma down a rabbit trail of descriptions of how the different Quaker sects developed. Thelma Jackson was the quintessential teacher.

"The Pleasant Hill Shaker Village is a National Historic Landmark. It was built in 1805, grew to a membership of three hundred people who worked 1,800 acres of land for almost half a century. That's where I came upon the only other mention of the village wiped out in the Indian raid. I found a Bible there the Shakers called the Carthage Bible."

The Bible was a big, leather-bound King James Bible, kept in a glass case because the pages were so fragile.

"They called it the Carthage Bible because of what was printed on the blank page in the front of the book. Under the words 'Carthage Angels' was a list of seventeen names. Below them were the words, 'Please, please forgive us. Mary Whitt, 7 October, 1830."

Thelma reached out again to the pile of information from the manila envelope and searched through it until she found a single sheet of typing paper.

"I copied the names down," she said, holding out the sheet. "And I never found these names connected to any descendants I tried to trace, which would make sense if they were killed in a massacre."

Sam took the sheet and began to read.

"'Forgive us,'" Charlie mused. "That's kind of an odd thing to say, don't you think? Us who?"

"And why only seventeen names?" Malachi asked.

"Surely there were more than seventeen people in the settlement."

"Maybe those were the names of Mary's children," Charlie said.

"They had big families, but seventeen …?"

"Not just her kids," Sam said, looking up from the sheet. "Only three of the names here are the same as hers — Jonah Whitt, Hannah Whitt and Ruth Whitt. And they could have been Mary Whitt's brother and sisters."

Charlie took the sheet from Sam and scanned down the names, wondering what Mary Whitt had done. What heinous sin had she committed that she was begging for forgiveness from people who'd been dead for thirty-five years?

Chapter Sixteen

RAYLYNN BENNETT WAS PROBABLY the only human being in all of Nowhere County who thought the Jabberwock was the best thing that had ever happened to her.

At least she had until E.J. had gone out to Judd Perkins's farm all by himself, which he shouldn't have done, which she should not have *let* him do but she had been distracted and then … Then.

But before that, before the bottom fell out of her whole world, there had been a glorious couple of weeks where every fantasy she had ever dared to dream had come true.

The Monster was gone. *Gone.*

She had cried when the hope first grabbed hold of her — that if nobody could leave Nowhere County maybe *nobody who was outside the county could come back*, she had cried. Sobbed.

And E.J. had misunderstood.

He had found her sitting alone in the pharmacy room, perched on the stool she used to get boxes off the top shelf because she wasn't very tall and neither was E.J. He had found her there after he'd returned from the trip out to see the Jabberwock stretched across the county line, in the van loaded with Malachi and Viola Tackett, Sam, Fish, Abby Clayton, Liam and that woman whose name was Charlie. The one E.J. looked at with the same longing in his gaze she was sure was in her own gaze when she looked at him.

He had opened the door and reached in just to flip off the light that he thought he had accidentally left on, when he saw her. Or maybe heard her.

"Raylynn?"

And she'd tried to hold it in, tried not to cry, but it was too big and she was too full, so she said nothing, just continued to sob quietly.

He had crossed the room to her, smelling vaguely of antiseptic and dog poop, which were not pleasant aromas to other people, but no one else was Raylynn Bennett.

"Hey, there. It's okay. Whatever it is, it'll be gone in a little while. Blew in here on a storm and it'll blow right back out on another one. You'll see."

He had put his arm around her shoulders, brotherly affection, and hugged her.

She had only cried the harder because she couldn't tell him that she wasn't crying because she was upset by the Jabberwock. She was crying in gratitude for it. The Jabberwock was a fence. Her father was on one side of it and she was on the other. For how long, she didn't know. But every second it lasted was a joy and wonder too big to hold inside.

He had gone to Clarksville, Indiana — on the other side of the Ohio River from Louisville, Kentucky — the day before, said he would stay with her older sister Eloise for the night and be back before noon.

She had gone home to the empty house that night from work at the clinic, went from room to room, screaming obscenities at him. So grateful for the solitude, the brief reprieve in her life of torment. She'd been glad of the storm that came up that night, the brief storm everybody thought had caused the Jabberwock. She'd been grateful because it had been so powerful it ripped at the shutters on the house, the ones her father had taken such care to paint and replace for the spring.

It had torn one off on the front of the house and left the other dangling. And after it was over, she'd gone out and ripped the other one off, too. Had to use the claw hammer from his toolbox to pull out the last of the screws that bound the hinge to the wall. Then she had banged the shutters against the house until they were nothing more than torn-up pieces of broken wood.

And every time she beat the shutter against the side of the house or the porch railings she imagined she was slamming it into his ugly face, breaking his nose, bursting his lip. Knocking out his teeth.

Every blow was a blow at her father. And she had slept well that night, as she only slept when he wasn't home. When he wasn't likely to appear in the gloom of her room, saying he "needed some loving.'"

She sometimes wondered if he had done the same with her older sister, if that's why she had run off and got married at sixteen, had moved away to Louisville. But she had never asked, and Daddy had seen to it she didn't have the same opportunities, scaring away anybody who took the slightest interest in her.

And there were few of those, of course.

She reached down unconsciously and pulled down the sleeve of her blouse that covered the raw red scar patches of psoriasis on her elbows. One good look at those, and the boys didn't need her father's threatening looks to keep their distance.

The morning after J-Day when the Jabberwock had

deposited the crowd of sick people in the parking lot outside and next door in front of the Dollar General Store, Raylynn had awakened with a surge of hope that maybe, *maybe*, the Jabberwock was still there. Still on guard. Still keeping her safe.

And it had been.

Every Jabberwock day for a week, she had awakened in fear and only relaxed when she got to work at the clinic and saw the faces of the people for whom the fence of the Jabberwock was not the lifesaver it was to Raylynn.

As one day piled up on top of another after J-Day, she had watched in love and admiration as E.J. stepped up to the plate and did what he didn't want to do or know how to do or was trained to do.

He'd done it anyway because that was the kind of man he was. And she had loved him more for it every day. And then Judd Perkins had called to say that something was wrong with his Great Pyrenees, Buster, and E.J. had gone to the Perkins farm to tend to the dog. The rabid dog.

E.J. had saved two little girls from certain death in the jaws of the crazed beast. Had sacrificed himself for them. And now he lay on a hospital bed in a makeshift hospital room in the clinic, with his leg a gory wound.

And the rabies virus in his veins.

When Raylynn'd heard Rusty cry out for his mother yesterday afternoon, she'd raced from the front desk to E.J.'s room, where Rusty was trying to hold E.J.'s heaving body on the bed.

Then Sam and Malachi and the others had arrived and she'd hung back, watching in horror from the shadows. The seizure passed. When she'd asked Sam if the seizure had hurt E.J., Sam'd said it hadn't "done any damage," but Raylynn knew that for the evasion it was.

They'd all left then. She sat alone with E.J. as he slept. Then he came to and when he did, he'd …

He had asked her …

E.J. had been afraid he might bite her or somebody else and infect them. Then he had broken, cried, begged her not to let him die of rabies.

And she had agreed.

She had promised.

She would keep that promise.

She allowed herself the luxury of tears for a few minutes now, sitting on the closed lid of the toilet with the water running in the sink to mask the sound. Then she grabbed hold of herself and stifled the tears, stood and splashed water into her face from the full basin and didn't even glance at her reflection in the mirror. She hadn't been able to look at herself in the mirror, look herself in the eye, since she'd promised E.J. yesterday that she would help him die.

She had looked it up in E.J.'s textbooks the day he was bitten, had read everything she could find there about rabies.

It had been the most horrifying tour through hell she could ever have imagined. But the salient point she clung to now, that E.J. had impressed upon her repeatedly, was that the incubation time for the rabies virus could be anywhere from a week to a year! It could take months for the first symptoms to appear. But once symptoms *did* appear, the end was certain. After the onset of symptoms, the disease was fatal *one hundred percent of the time.*

The week line-in-the-sand was the jumping-off point. If the antivenom were administered within a week of the bite, *before* any symptoms developed, the survival rate was better than ninety percent. After that, every day was a crapshoot. Would symptoms appear today? The week was the only guaranteed safety zone, and E.J. had made her promise she would not let him suffer past a week.

She had only a couple of days left to do what she had to do.

Raylynn rubbed her face hard with the towel hanging on the rack, scrubbed at it. Then she turned off the tap and stepped out into the hallway. She could hear Sam's voice in the breakroom, talking to Thelma Jackson, Malachi and Charlie. Raylynn slipped silently down the hallway past the almost-closed door, past the front of the clinic where there were no patients right now in the waiting room to the big exam room on the end. That's where Sam hung up what she called her pretending-I'm-a-doctor white lab coat.

Slipping her hand into the pocket of the coat, Raylynn found the bottle of pills. The pills Malachi had given Sam to use to alleviate E.J.'s pain. The don't-ask-me-where-I-got-this bottle of pure oxycontin.

She quickly unscrewed the lid and dropped two pills out into her palm from the bottle. Stood for a moment thinking, then dropped out one more.

She didn't know how much it would take for the dose to be fatal, but she couldn't take so many that Sam would notice they were gone. In a real hospital, where there might possibly be drug-addicted patients or staff, narcotics were locked away. The only locked safe in the Healthy Pets Veterinary Clinic was where E.J. kept his "horse tranquilizer" because he'd read somewhere that there were idiots out there stupid enough to shoot up with it. Sam didn't use the safe for the oxycontin. She carried a bottle in her pocket and Raylynn could only hope that Sam didn't know exactly how many pills were in it. After all, it wasn't a prescription bottle with the number of tablets printed clearly on the label, and Malachi had promised an "unlimited supply" of the drugs, so she didn't have to keep track — he'd provide more when this bottle ran low.

Raylynn had to find out how many pills it took for a fatal dose. And then, she had to find a way to come by *twice* that amount. E.J. wouldn't die alone. When she gave E.J. the pills to end his life, she intended to have a handful of her own to take when he took his.

They would die together.

Chapter Seventeen

SAM WAS LISTENING to Thelma Jackson's recounting of the history of Gideon and the town that'd sat on the same spot a hundred years before it when she heard the commotion out in the hallway and her gut yanked into a knot. It was a crisis of some kind. An emergency. And odds were she was about to be asked to function as if she were a doctor — any number of doctors, actually, when you counted the illnesses, injuries and diagnoses she'd been required to make just like she was a fully staffed medical clinic instead of a lone EPN, hanging out here by herself without even a veterinarian to help her make medical decisions.

A timid knock announced that Raylynn was on the other side, loath to interrupt what she understood were probably the most important conversations in the whole county. But she'd knocked, so it must be—

The door opened slightly and Raylynn peeked into the room.

"Sam ... I hate to interrupt but ... we got ... Skeeter Burkett and Ed Reynolds just brought in ... a body. Skeeter pulled it out of the river." She paused, took a breath and whispered urgently, "Sam, I think it might be Reverend Norman's girl, Hayley."

The others in the room turned to Raylynn in alarm. Everybody knew Hayley was missing. Her father, Reverend Duncan Norman, had questioned just about every person who'd been at Viola's kangaroo court at the courthouse yesterday, saying he couldn't find her.

When Hayley'd ridden the Jabberwock to the Middle of Nowhere on J-Day, she had been on her way to Lexington to get an abortion. She'd told Sam that, but Sam suspected she hadn't shared it with anybody else. Like everybody who took a Jabberwock trip, her vehicle had vanished in a puff of smoke. And apparently she had taken the family's only other vehicle to go wherever it was she'd gone on Saturday. Members of Rev. Norman's small congregation had been driving him around so he could look for her.

Sam didn't stop to question why Skeeter and Ed had brought the body to the veterinary clinic, specifically to Sam. She was all there was, the only medical care of any kind in the county, and by default she'd somehow become the go-to person for anybody in crisis. Viola Tackett may have set herself up as the "law" in Nowhere County, but without lifting a finger, Sam Sheridan had become the resident "authority." The one who would have responded if you'd dialed 911.

Gratefully, Malachi stepped in to orchestrate what came next, directing Thelma and Raylynn to stay inside while he and Sam went outside with Skeeter to the front parking lot, where a large lump of something lay covered in a tarp in the bed of Ed Reynolds's pickup truck. Charlie had tagged along with them and Malachi didn't challenge her.

"Ain't no way to be sure it's Hayley," Skeeter said softly.

He didn't look good, like maybe he was about to throw up. "You'll see."

When Ed pulled back the tarp, Sam did see and she took an involuntary step back. Charlie squeaked out a little scream and turned away. The woman who lay in a wet heap had been dead several days, and the ravages of decomposition would have made identifying her unpleasant in the best of circumstances. But even if she'd been fished out of the water five minutes after she went in, she still wouldn't have been recognizable. Her face was gone, nothing on the front of her head but the crushed remains of a nose, mouth and eyes. It looked like she had slammed into a brick wall face-first going sixty miles an hour.

"Found her in the river downstream from Scott's Ridge. I only thought it was Hayley because—" Skeeter pointed to the ring stuck on the pudgy little finger of her right hand. It was a small gold band with a raised disc the size of a dime with an inlaid cross and the letters PHPC. Praying Hands Pentecostal Church. "Maybe they's a lot of rings like that out there, I don't know. But …" He gestured to the huge bloated body. "I mean … look at her. Ain't any other girl I know in Nowhere County fat as that."

Yes, it was Hayley Norman alright.

Sam shook her head to clear it, but could do nothing about the tears that had formed instantly in her eyes. She felt a hand on her shoulder. Malachi patted gently.

"Sorry you got stuck with all this," he said.

She wanted to melt in a puddle. Hayley Norman's dead, mutilated body was bad enough without the emotional upheaval of having to deal with Malachi Tackett on top of it. But she couldn't just shrug his hand off, much as she wanted to. Except, of course, she didn't want to. Which was the reason she needed to.

She shook her head again, heard fill-the-awkward-silence words tumble out of her mouth in a whisper.

"She was pregnant."

Malachi's eyebrows shot up but he made no comment.

"That's where she was going on J-Day. To Lexington to … get rid of it."

"But she wound up in the Middle of Nowhere instead," Charlie said, and Sam realized then that Charlie had stepped up to stand beside her. She was so grateful she almost reached out to clasp Charlie's hand.

"On Saturday, Hayley asked me to do it. To … you know …"

"Perform an abortion," Charlie finished for her.

"She was devastated when I said no. She must have been so desperate … what else could she do but …?"

Though Sam didn't think anyone had ever done it, the Scott's Ridge Overlook had always seemed to be a Lover's Leap kind of location. Jump off and it's a drop straight down into the river — into the *big rocks* clotting the river beneath the overlook. Not survivable.

"She didn't leap off Scott's Ridge," Malachi said. "She didn't commit suicide."

How did he know she was thinking …? She just looked at him questioningly.

"You don't get injuries like that jumping off a cliff, not even if you land on your face." He gestured, keeping his voice low. "Both the front and the back of her head are bashed in. Hard to do that in a fall unless you bounce off something on the way down and she didn't. She didn't kill herself. Somebody beat her to death."

Sam sucked in a gasp.

"You're saying somebody *murdered* …?"

"She tell you who the father of the baby was?"

"No, just called him Sugar Bear."

"Hayley was what? Sixteen?" Charlie said. "Safe money's on Sugar Bear is a married man and wanted her to get the abortion, maybe even gave her the money to pay for it, and when she couldn't … If Liam were here, that's where he'd start looking."

"But he's not." Sam heard sadness wrapped up in anger in her own voice and she was glad of it.

"And the 'law' in this county right now doesn't give a rip," Malachi said and she was glad he said it so she didn't have to.

"What are we supposed to do with … where do we take the body?" Skeeter wanted to know.

"Bascum's," Sam said. The failed funeral home was a growing concern now.

"You need any help?" Malachi asked Sam and she gave him a blank look. "You know … telling her family."

The bottom dropped out of Sam's belly and she felt her knees go weak. She didn't wobble, though; she was proud of that. But she only shook her head because she didn't trust herself to speak.

Yep, that job had fallen to her, too. Notifying the families of the dead. Who else was there to do it?

Where did it end?

It didn't. Never would unless the Breakfast Club could come up with more answers than they had right now.

"I'll go with you," Charlie said softly beside her and Sam did take her hand then and squeezed it.

"Thanks, but I don't need any help."

"Don't be ridiculous, of course you do."

Sam had never loved Charlie more than she did at that moment.

"I'm coming with you and we best go right now before news hits the phone tree."

"Are you going to tell them ... all of it?" Malachi asked.

She looked from Malachi to Charlie. Should she share with Hayley's parents that she had been pregnant? That she had been murdered?

What was the point?

She was grateful that Malachi agreed.

"*When* we get out of here," he looked pointedly from Sam to Charlie and back to Sam, "then maybe we'll need to share all we know about a lot of things." He paused and she watched his face. He appeared to put something together in his head before he continued. "Even then ... I don't think the part about Hayley will matter. I think maybe justice has already been served."

Sam had no idea what he was talking about and both she and Charlie started to ask, but he held up his hand in a "not-now" gesture. "Why make the death of their only child harder on the Normans than it's already going to be?"

Charlie nodded agreement.

Malachi gestured toward Skeeter and Ed Reynolds — standing off to the side by themselves. "I'll give them a hand with the body."

"I guess we need to give Lester a call, give him a heads-up," Charlie said.

A rhyme Sam had heard from her grandmother flashed into her mind. "Be the job great or small, if you do it too well, you get stuck with it all." That had certainly been the case with Sam in the past two weeks and it had happened to Lester Peetree, too. Lester ran the hardware store, had gone to Charlie's after ... after what happened with Abby Clayton, and took the kiln door off the hinges. The most remarkable thing about Lester Peetree was that there was absolutely nothing remarkable about him at all.

He was quintessentially ordinary. Except he wasn't. Though he had an easily forgettable face and a soft voice, Lester Peetree was a *go-to guy*, the man you could always depend on in a crisis. Not flashy, tended to hover out there beyond the circle of "people in charge," Lester would crawl over ten miles of razor blades and rusty can lids to keep a promise. At forty-seven, he shaved his head to hide creeping baldness, and always wore long-sleeved shirts to cover the scars from shrapnel wounds he'd gotten in Vietnam. Though it was rumored he'd come back from the war with a pocketful of medals for valor, it was hard for Sam to imagine him as the "certifiable badass" Liam said he'd been, a sniper with dozens of confirmed kills.

Lester had been friends with Herb Bascum, the mortician who owned the funeral home that'd closed years ago. They'd gone to boot camp together after they'd been drafted in 1967. When the Jabberwock claimed its first victim on J-Day, they'd taken Willie Cochran's body to Bascum's and Lester'd unlocked the building, made sure the refrigeration units that'd been sitting unused all these years still worked. The funeral home was only a couple of doors down from the hardware store and Herb had given Lester a key so he could use the back room there to store bags of fertilizer. Lester'd kept the electricity turned on.

In the new normal of post J-Day reality in Nowhere County, Lester Peetree was now in charge of the growing population of bodies in refrigerated drawers in Bascum's basement.

"Let me go make sure the self-appointed veterinary clinic manager can hang out with Raylynn for a while," Charlie said. "I'll call Lester and be right back."

Sam was grateful for the time Charlie took to arrange things for Merrie. She needed the few minutes to get her emotional ducks in a row.

What should she say? What *could* she say?

She hadn't been trained for something like this, any more than she'd been trained for the other tasks she'd performed with a gun to her head in the past two weeks. Falling back on a half-hour lecture once on delivering bad news, she concentrated on the basics. Short simple sentences. No hemming and hawing. Say what you have to say kindly, but unequivocally. Then just listen.

Okay, she could do that.

A sardonic laugh died in her throat. Right. Like she had a choice.

Chapter Eighteen

SHEP CLAYTON WAS ONLY EVER around Abby's Uncle Virgil, her mama's brother, at cock fights. Last time Shep seen him, Virgil had started a brawl when his bird lost, busted a chair over some fella's head. Fella was still in a bad way, or so Shep'd heard.

Abby'd told Shep and her crazy older brother Claude, yesterday, that they was s'posed to do something about them as was making trouble for the Jabberwock — Cotton Jackson, Stuart McClintock and Pete Rutherford's daughter, Jolene. Soon's she did, Claude had called his uncle, asked Virgil could he round up some boys and could they meet at Virgil's house at noon today. Didn't say nothing about why.

Shep, Abby and most of Abby's kin — aunts, uncles, cousins and such — lived in and around Poorfolk Hollow in southwest Nowhere County, on the far side of Hollow Tree Ridge. Her mama'd been Winona Hannaker, and over the years a whole passel of that side of the family had spread out 'til some of them was on the Drayton County side of the hollow. Them folks hadn't lost nothing. 'Course they was well aware of what'd happened in Nowhere County — more'n half the family was there. Except they wasn't there. Not anymore, they wasn't.

Virgil's wife, Pauline, had laid out a spread and Shep could smell the apple pie from the front porch.

"Ya'll want to pass them black-eyed peas on down to this side of the table," said Claude, sitting there in the big chair at the end across from his uncle, taking it as his right and due soon's he walked in the door. Shep didn't think none of his kin had visited Claude when he was in that nut house, so it'd been years since they'd set eyes on him, but now that he was home, he acted like he'd never left, like all the rest of the family'd ought to do for him because he was Winona's oldest. It was clear quick that didn't none of them want anything to do with Claude. He always had been odd, and odd had over time turned into peculiar in a bad way and after a while the family was … say the truth of it, scared to be around him. Wasn't nobody shed no tears when they heard he'd been locked away for hacking his drug-dealing partners to death with a hatchet, and Shep was sure wasn't none of them doing no happy dance when they found out he'd come back home.

Shep was only here cause Abby'd told him to come. It wasn't up to Shep no more what he said or didn't say, nor what he done. Abby was the one deciding things now. The Abby that was in his head who didn't have Abby's bird-chirp voice was calling the shots. Shep was sitting on the sidelines. She'd told Shep not to pay no mind to that Stuart McClintock fella as had come by to visit him on Saturday evening. Said he was married to Charlie Ryan — him a black man and her white. That absolutely was not right and Abby'd said as much, but that wasn't why she didn't want Shep to listen to what the man had to say. She said it was Charlie McClintock coming home that'd caused all the trouble in the first place! Abby said the Jabberwock had been waiting for *her and her friends* — and everybody else in the county just got locked up right along with them.

The whole thing was Charlie McClintock's fault!

Abby told Shep that Charlie's husband, Stuart, had flown in from Chicago and was digging around in things that didn't concern him. She said Shep'd ought to run him off the way he'd run off a weasel that got in the chicken house.

Then Claude Letcher'd came strolling into Shep and Abby's house yesterday — the house that wasn't no house no more. Abby started talking to her big brother outta Shep's mouth, told him all kinda things Shep didn't know about what had happened and why. And who was responsible. And what she wanted him and Claude to do about it. She got real specific — which meant they had to lay their hands on some guns. Ordinarily, that wouldn't have been no thang. Shep had all kinda guns — shot rabbits and squirrels and deer to put meat on the table like everybody else in the county did. Shep's guns had vanished with Abby and the house.

But her kin had guns. That's why him and Claude had come to see her Uncle Virgil.

And now they sat there at the table in Uncle Virgil's kitchen, talking with Claude and Abby's cousins, Billy Ray and Doodlebug Hannaker, and a couple of friends, Ronnie Potter and Jim Bob Claywell — who'd helped Shep run the McGinty tractor into a creek when they was drunk teenagers. Ronnie and Jim Bob both lived in Nowhere County but they'd been away — likely out somewhere selling weed — and come home to find their families gone, same as Shep had.

'Cept their houses was just empty, not old. And their wives hadn't come back like Abby had, so she was right there inside Shep's head. He sat now listening to her speak out his mouth, asking after Doodlebug's youngest, Effie, who had some kind of heart problem, and wanting to know if Jim Bob's mama's gout was still bothering her and did Billy Ray ever find his bird dog that'd run off.

"I ain't had no home-cooked food in a month of Sundays," Claude said, piling his plate high with fried chicken, mashed potatoes and gravy, fried okra and black-eyed peas.

"That what you come back for, Claude?" asked Billy Ray. "Missed cornbread and buttermilk, didja, locked away in the nut house like you was?"

Claude's cousin speaking to him like that had ought to have got under Claude's skin, but it didn't.

"I come back because this here's my home and I got as much right to be here as anybody else at this table." Then he glanced at Shep. "Least that's what I thought I'd come back for. But when I showed up and found things the way they is, I figured out I come here for some other reason I didn't even know, some" — he stopped and grinned — "higher purpose."

"Just what purpose might *that* be?" Doodlebug asked.

Uncle Virgil chided his sons. "Now, boys, you act like you ain't glad to see your cousin." Which they weren't and weren't putting up a very good show of hiding it.

"Any of you interested in getting all the people back who's disappeared?" Claude asked, with his mouth full of mashed potatoes. That was a conversation stopper. You coulda heard a mouse in house shoes tiptoeing across a cotton ball in the silence that followed.

Jim Bob lived in Frogtown with his wife and two boys. Ronnie and his wife, Becky Sue, lived with his parents and sister on Elkhorn Road. All them people was gone now.

"'Course we are!" Jim Bob said. He looked around the

table. "It ain't like we ain't been trying! We all went to the law and reported it." He sneered at Claude. "You think you can do a better job of getting help than we did, you go on ahead — and they'll throw you in a cell with the Caswell brothers, Truman Pettigrew, and I don't even know who all else. Or haul you off in an ambulance like they done them folks from Wisconsin who come looking for their granny."

Some of the Nowhere people who'd lost families didn't take it real well that the state police didn't do nothing. They'd got ugly about it and got locked up. And they was some away-from-here folks who kept going back and forth across the county line until they gave up because they got sick — vomiting and nosebleeds and such.

"It's powerful queer," Aunt Pauline said, filling up her husband's glass of ice tea. "The law comes and they see it. They see ain't nobody there, houses empty, everything gone. They 'investigate' and write it down and then they never come back with no help."

"Their remembering's gone," Uncle Virgil said.

Aunt Pauline nodded. "They come down with the forgets and don't know nothing about what they seen, throw their reports in the trash, I guess, 'cause they sound so crazy."

"When you go back to ask why didn't they do what they said they'd do, they look at you like you's the one lost your mind," Uncle Virgil said.

"Them Wisconsin folks musta seen that they granny and everybody else was missing and then forgot they seen it," Aunt Pauline said. "So they come back a whole bunch of times. The forgetting must be hard on you 'cause after awhile them folks was half dead."

"We don't need all them outsiders to fix our problem,"

Claude said, piling another helping of okra on his plate. "It's up to us to do it ourselves, our way."

"And what way is that, Claude?" Jim Bob asked. "You know where they at, do you — all them missing people?" His voice dropped to a whisper. "You know where my Jenny is — Derek and Jason?"

Shep told 'em then. "Abby talks to me." He got the expected disbelieving, sympathetic looks. He tapped his temple. "She's in my head. You can believe me or no, but she says all them people that's gone is still right where they was — we just can't see them."

"That's crazy!" Doodlebug said.

"Any crazier than a whole county full of people vanishing in the first place?" Claude said.

"And nobody remembering what they seen here soon's they cross the county line?" Shep said.

Didn't nobody have an answer for that.

"They's a thing called a Jabberwock's got them."

"You done lost your mind, Shep." Jim Bob shook his head — sad-like, not mad.

"The Jabberwock told my Abby it's gonna let them all go."

"*When?*" Ronnie demanded, his voice cracking with emotion. "Becky Sue's pregnant and the baby was due a week ago."

"Not when ... *if.*"

"If what?" Billy Ray asked.

"If we keep folks from meddling in the Jabberwock's bidness," Claude said. "It don't want *all* them people it took. Never did want 'em all. It just wants three of them, but it's gonna hang onto every mother's child in Nowhere County unless ..."

"Unless what?" Aunt Pauline asked.

"Unless we leave it alone. They's folks buttin' in what

don't concern them. One of them's Cotton Jackson and another is Pete Rutherford's daughter. Third one's an outsider, a black man married to a white woman." Claude spit on the floor after he said it.

"How are we supposed to stop 'em from meddling?" Uncle Virgil wanted to know.

"Shoot 'em," Claude said, matter-of-fact as *pass the cornbread*. "That's why me and Shep is here. We ain't got no hardware no more. Everything of Shep's …" He let the sentence dangle. Nobody needed an explanation. "You still got yours, though. And we need to borrow some."

"You want us to supply you with guns so's you can walk out that door with 'em and *shoot* somebody — that what you sayin'?" Uncle Virgil was having a hard time wrapping his mind around a request like that.

Claude smiled, revealing his hoary mouth with missing and rotted teeth.

"Yup. That's what I'm sayin'."

They was a rumble of thunder outside, rattled the window panes. Shep wondered if maybe Abby'd done it, made it thunder. He suspected she could if she wanted to. He suspected there wasn't nothing anymore that Abby couldn't do.

Chapter Nineteen

"I *HATE* FORREST GUMP!" Douglas Taylor said, and kicked a rock down the steep grade of the hillside to watch it plunk into the creek.

"Awe, come on," said Rusty Sheridan. He nudged a bigger rock with his toe to loosen it, then shoved it off to dive in behind Douglas's. "It's like one of the best movies *ever* … that part where he's on the shrimp boat and he sees Lieutenant Dan on the dock and he just—"

"I didn't say I hated the movie. I said I hated Forrest Gump — the guy, the character."

Rusty knew Douglas didn't really hate the movie *or* the character. He hated the character's *haircut* — and that was certainly understandable! That haircut had made Douglas Taylor the laughing stock of Carlisle Middle School. Well, not just the haircut. Douglas already had a couple of strikes against him. He was — what was it Rusty'd heard Fish call Mrs. Gillespie that time Fish was mostly sober? *Rotund.* That was Douglas alright — rotund, with rosy, round cheeks. And his totally clueless mother actually called him "Dougie" in public. *At school!* She engaged in a lot of public affection, too, which landed Douglas the nick-names Huggie Dougie and the Hugable Dougable. Rusty's mom had said Douglas's mother was "half a bubble off plumb" and Rusty'd told himself to remember that phrase so he could use it to describe his friends when they acted stupid. Douglas's mother was more than just stupid, though. The way she acted about Douglas, wouldn't let him play in the mud, for crying out loud, or drink out of a water hose, said she was protecting "her baby" from germs. That time he and Douglas had climbed a tree and she called the fire department to get Douglas down — the look in her panicked eyes, Rusty believed that day that she was genuinely crazy.

But even if the woman was only clueless, she'd outdone herself in cluelessness a couple of months ago. Rusty was sure it qualified as some form of child abuse. After she saw the movie, Claire Taylor had told the barber to cut *little Dougie's* hair "just like Forrest Gump's."

Rusty stopped, felt like he'd been kicked in the belly. How long would it be before the reality of J-Day was no longer shocking? How long would it take before it was just ho-hum: "Yeah, that's the way life used to be but not anymore, we're *stuck here* — bummer." Well, it would take longer than two weeks for Rusty Sheridan to stop feeling nauseous every time he thought about it! And he thought about it *a lot*, because it changed *everything*.

It didn't matter anymore how Douglas wore his hair, or if his mother hugged him in public or if … nothing like that mattered now that he and the rest of the kids in Nowhere County couldn't go back to school in Beaufort County in the fall. Not as long as the Jabberwock stood in their way. And how long would that be?

"I think Forrest Gump is a … a … jackass," Douglas continued, and was right pleased with himself for being able/willing to use the word. Rusty tried to act suitably impressed. Douglas was only ten and didn't have a really firm grasp on profanity, its nature and its uses. He only knew he wasn't supposed to say certain words and so, duh, those were the words he tried to drop into any and every conversation.

At twelve, Rusty was far more advanced in the skill of cursing. When his mother, Sam, was out making her rounds all over the county as a home health nurse, Rusty used to stand in front of the bathroom mirror and practice dropping cuss words in between the syllables of regular words — so it sounded smooth and natural when he did it around his friends, like he talked that way all the time. He didn't, of course, and in point of fact neither did any of them. Boy talk at home and boy talk among friends was—

Friends. He wouldn't be seeing his Beaufort County friends until … unless—

The Jabberwock.

He shivered and tuned back in to Douglas's prattle, which was more or less nonstop, a background noise that Rusty mostly ignored.

"— time to grow out by then." Douglas grabbed a hunk of his blond hair — the part that was long enough to grab.

Forrest Gump was a great movie and all that — and Rusty would watch Tom Hanks take a dump! — but surely no one would dispute that his haircut was nightmare material. Shaved down to like an eighteenth of an inch from his ears halfway to the top of his head. The hair on the top was hardly long enough to need combing. Well, except for the two years when Forrest was running back and forth across the country — didn't cut his hair and grew a beard.

In the beard department … Rusty had found two black hairs on his upper lip last fall and had been so excited he'd named them. But so far, none of their friends had shown up to join the party. He checked every morning in his mother's magnifying makeup mirror.

Rusty's hair wasn't as long as Forrest's had gotten then, either, but it was thick — and curly, which he *hated!* At least his mother let him wear it long-*ish*, down into his collar. It wasn't red anymore — thank you, Lord! — like it had been when he was a toddler. That's when he'd become "Rusty." First name Russell, red hair — Rusty was inevitable. Gratefully, his hair color had darkened as he got older and now it was just brown, though in bright sunlight you could still see red in it.

Oh, he thought his mother's red hair was gorgeous. She looked beautiful with it hanging down smooth around her face. But she was a girl. Red hair was fine for girls. If it was real. Douglas's mother dyed her hair a shade of red Rusty's mother called "a Sears color" — meaning it wasn't a color found in nature. It'd been blonde when she and Douglas lived across the street from Rusty in the Ridge, with her husband — what was his name? Rusty couldn't remember. He'd been the second one while they lived in that house and now she'd married somebody else altogether and had moved in with him. Which was why Rusty's mother had to bring him out into the boonies past Twig this morning to spend time with Douglas. It'd been her idea and Rusty knew why. She felt bad that his life had pretty much fallen apart, but things were tough for everybody now. She thought she had been neglecting him ever since …

The Jabberwock.

It was out here somewhere. The Beaufort County line was only about half a mile away. Which was why Douglas's mother had strictly forbidden him to play in this part of the woods. Which, of course, was why Douglas had demanded they play here — you got your little victories wherever you could. Douglas had wanted to go see the Jabberwock, but Rusty put the kibosh on that, told him you couldn't see "a mirage" in the trees — which wasn't strictly true. You could if you knew what to look for. Rusty knew. He'd seen it lots of times. But more important, he'd seen what it could do lots of times, had been with his mother at the clinic in the Middle of Nowhere when they had an "incoming." Somebody who had accidentally stumbled into it — he supposed things like that happened. It was more likely, though, that they'd decided to make a break for it. But it really didn't matter what their reason for challenging the Jabberwock was, the result was always the same — the just-shoot-me experience of projectile vomiting in front of people. Or maybe just suffering the mother of all nosebleeds. Or going blind and deaf. There were lots of menu items. But the single worst thing Rusty could imagine was throwing up with an audience. He would rather die.

What if he was sitting on the bench in the bus shelter up-chucking on his brand new Air Jordans and Whitney Malone was there and she had to leap out of the way so the puke wouldn't splatter on her? He was picturing the horror of that when he heard the sound. The *rattle*. But by then it was too late. The rattlesnake had already struck.

Chapter Twenty

When Hayley was little, she thought her father was Atticus Finch from the movie *To Kill a Mockingbird*. They'd taken her to see it and when Gregory Peck walked into the kitchen in the first part of the movie, Hayley had disrupted the whole theater pointing at him and crying, "Daddy, Daddy."

Duncan Norman looked a little like Gregory Peck, he'd always supposed. Dark hair, thick eyebrows, a carved face, tall, thin lips more accustomed to frowns and severe looks than smiles. He had always thought that's where the resemblance lay, in the facial expressions, not the structure. Atticus Finch was a man who stood his ground for his principles, just like Duncan Norman stood his ground for his spiritual ones. Both men were willing to fight for what they believed in, were not cowed by opposition.

Both men adored their little girls.

Duncan heard a sound come from his throat, a kind of strangled sob he didn't even recognize as his own, though it must have been.

He thought about Atticus reading to Scout when she

was little so often she had learned to read before she entered first grade, and had gotten in trouble for it. He had read to Hayley, too, when she was little. Every night. Bible stories and *Grimms' Fairy Tales* and *The Hobbit*. She hadn't gotten in trouble because of it but she had gotten a bald spot.

His eyes swam with tears at the memory of the little thing — pale and thin, with all manner of congenital digestive issues that made processing food a challenge — and no hair on the top of her head. He and Miriam and the doctors were convinced it was yet another manifestation of the malfunctioning gall bladder or pancreas or liver. She was hospitalized. Batteries of tests turned up only the usual suspects that would eventually doom her to a life of obesity. Nothing indicated a cause for her hair falling out.

Then Duncan figured it out one night as she sat in his lap in the platform rocker, so still, her breathing so slow and even that he often thought she had fallen asleep. But she was absolutely alert, heard every word as he read to her ... resting his chin on the top of her head. His chin with the day's growth of beard. Which was systematically sanding off her thin growth of blonde hair.

They'd all laughed about it.

He even teased her about it now, sometimes, asking if she'd checked the top of her head for hair lately.

The image of the little girl with a bald spot was overlaid by the image of the ... the ...

Why hadn't he listened to Sam Sheridan? She'd warned him, told him not to go barreling down to the funeral home, rushing to his daughter's side.

He remembered her words distinctly and the intensity with which she said them.

"Your daughter is the girl whose picture you carry in your wallet. That's Hayley. That's the Hayley you want to remember. Please, please don't spoil that image forever by—"

But he wouldn't listen. Stubborn. Defiant. Since he was *always right* — and the Reverend Duncan Norman was, after all, always right — he didn't listen to the warning, gave in to the horror of need in his chest to be with his little girl, to see her—

And he had seen.

He hadn't let Miriam go in. Thank God for that. He had made her wait in the car.

There was no face on the head of the person lying bloated and stinky on the metal tray.

No face. Her head bashed in *on both sides.*

A body, battered and bruised and broken.

He felt something wet in his hand and opened his clenched fist to see blood on his palms. He had squeezed his fingers into such a tight fist that his fingernails had cut into his flesh.

But there was no pain. Didn't feel a thing.

The pain in his chest, his belly, his heart, his whole soul was so great that he could have cut off his hand and he would have felt nothing at all.

"Duncan …?"

The words came in a soft voice from behind him. It was Miriam. There was such need in that lone word he wanted to turn and run away from her. Felt as if she were sucking all of who he was, his whole being out of himself with the power of her need to be comforted in her loss. Their loss.

But he was only able right now to feel his own loss. Maybe someday he would care about Miriam's but not right now.

"Later," he managed to croak. "I need to be alone now with the Lord."

He was standing by himself on the back porch, the murmur of voices coming from inside the house muted. But Duncan wasn't with the Lord. Not in that sense. Not in the sense of communing with the Almighty, basking in the joy of being a child of God. He was "with the Lord' only because the Lord was everywhere. But he was not in any kind of communion with the great I Am.

Right now, if he had come face to face with the great God Jehovah, he'd have screamed obscenities at Him.

His baby girl was dead. She had killed herself — flung herself off the Scott's Ridge Overlook onto the jagged rocks in the Rolling Fork River! Why? What had been so horribly wrong, so devastating that she would rather die than face it? He desperately wanted to know the answer to that question, would find out why if he had to search for the reason every day for the rest of his life!

But not now. Not today. Right now, he was so full of grief it shoved every other thought and intention out of his heart and mind.

God had taken his precious child.

On some level, Duncan Norman realized he was not the first father who had ever lost a daughter, that he was in no way unique and special in his pain, that he had no more right than any other mortal to question the will of the Almighty and His absolute right to exercise His will in whatever way suited Him.

He knew that. Understood it. But the cold, hard reality was that he flat-out didn't care. Didn't care about anything "spiritual" after Sam Sheridan and that other woman — Charlie something, the daughter of Sylvia Ryan, he thought — came to his door. He'd invited them in, the pain in Sam's eyes only mildly frightening him at first. After all, people came to see him all the time in pain, needing his comfort, needing the comfort of God that he could assure was theirs for the asking.

Then Sam had said Hayley's name.

Just said her name, and Duncan knew she was dead.

Only her name.

Miriam had not picked up on it, though, had rushed forward in the bit of awkward silence that followed Sam's statement that, "we have found Hayley." Miriam had relaxed in a heap, collapsed on the arm of the chair in the parlor, her body a study in relief.

"Thank you, Jesus!" she'd said. "We have been worried sick, imagining all kinds of horrible things. Thank you, Sam, for finding her. Where is she?"

And then Sam had said the words Duncan knew she'd say but that confused Miriam.

"Bascum's."

"What's Hayley doing at Bascum's? Why——?"

And when realization landed on Miriam, she backed up from it, cried out *no*, put her hands out in front of her as if she could physically hold back the reality of it. Then she went from zero to sixty on the hysteria scale, screaming "no, no, no!" and shaking her head frantically, absolutely refusing to hear the words that came after.

Hayley was at Bascum's because she was dead. Skeeter Burkett had found her body in the river.

Sam had paused then, in the profound silence that had fallen when he and Miriam were so shocked and horrified they were incapable of sound. "It appears she died Saturday night."

And then Miriam dissolved in a puddle.

Hayley had been dead for two days. All that time, all those minutes and hours in between then and now, when they were looking for her so frantically, turning over every stone, calling her friends ...

She had been in the river. Her cold, dead body had been in the river.

"Duncan … please."

Such need in Miriam's voice, it tore out his chest.

When he turned to her, he flashed on the movie, on Hayley crying out "Daddy," and he knew he must right now look like Atticus Finch had looked in the courtroom scene when he was cross-examining the redneck farmer who'd charged his client with rape.

"I said to leave me alone."

Harsh and cruel, the words sounded harsh and cruel. Because they were. But he didn't have anything in him to give. His faith, his belief, his hope, everything he had and was about had drained out of him when he learned his baby girl was dead. Now, when he needed faith, needed strength, needed the hope of his years of closeness to God, there was nowhere to go. He could do nothing but scrape at the bottom of an empty bucket. The sound the cup made on the metal at the bottom ground into his soul.

Duncan Norman turned then from his desperate, shattered wife and strode past her back into the kitchen, past people who spoke to him, he supposed, through the kitchen and living room to the stairs. He took them two at a time, up to Hayley's room.

Suddenly, if he didn't get to Hayley's room, if he didn't go there where her essence was—

The face. Gone. Smashed in. Crushed in.

Your little girl is the face you have in your wallet.

He should have listened. Dear God, how he wished he had listened.

He opened her door, stepped into the room, closed it behind him and leaned against it, panting. He was crying, too, he supposed. He couldn't tell. He could feel that his cheeks were wet and his shoulders were shaking, but there was no sound.

He sat down on the edge of her bed — it was unmade. He'd made Miriam leave it that way because there was something terrifyingly final about making up the bed before the child came home.

And — oh, God, forgive him! — he'd wanted Hayley to make it up when she got home. It was her job, after all, and he was determined to teach her to be responsible, to honor her obligations.

The bedspread that was half off the bed, hanging on the floor, was the bright red of the University of Louisville, with the insignia of the U of L cardinal — looking mean — emblazoned on the front.

There was never any doubt what Hayley Norman would be "when she grew up." She had never wavered. She had kept her dolls so wrapped up in bandages and Band-Aids they all looked like survivors of an earthquake.

Someday, Hayley Norman would be a doctor, she'd announced proudly when she couldn't have been more than six or seven years old. Now, at sixteen, almost seventeen, she'd walked that ambition back. She and her mother had already started pouring over University of Louisville Nursing School brochures and checking into the availability of financial aid.

Duncan Norman was a minister. His salary was barely enough to put food on the table and he had never been able to put a dime aside for Hayley's education.

Now, there'd be no education to pay for. Now ... he needed to begin considering how he was going to pay for her funeral.

He did cry then, put his head in his hands and sobbed. Cried until his sides ached and his throat was raw.

And that's why he found it. He reached out to pull

tissues from the box of them on Hayley's bedside table and only one tissue came out in his hand. The box wasn't full as it seemed to be. The lone tissue on the top rested on something else in the box. *Hid* something else in the box. He lifted the box and looked through the hole on the top. Inside was a narrow book with a leather cover. He had never seen the book before, had no idea where Hayley had gotten it. But it was obvious what it was. Printed in swirling cursive letters on the cover were the words: My Diary. Which explained why she'd hidden it in the tissue box. Bound within the pages of that book were his little girl's most private thoughts, her hopes and dreams and sorrows.

He pulled the volume almost reverently out of the box. What lay inside was private. He would never have dreamed of intruding on that privacy if Hayley had been alive. But now, he held in his hand the intimate thoughts of the little girl who would never be able to speak them, share them with her daddy.

His fingers trembled when he opened the book and began to read.

Chapter Twenty-One

Sam was quiet as she drove from Rev. Norman's house back to the animal hospital. She was anxious to check on E.J. They'd worked out shifts among the six of them — Sam, Charlie, Malachi, Judd Perkins, his daughter Doreen Jaggers and Raylynn — to sit with him because Sam didn't want him to be alone, not even for a minute. They had a long list of other volunteers they could tap into if the need arose. They hadn't yet needed the others because of Raylynn. She was omnipresent, in all the cracks, taking up all the slack. There's no way they could have pulled it off without Raylynn's help, not with all the other assorted catastrophes she and Charlie and Malachi had to attend to.

There'd been quite a few medical semi-emergencies. Becky Sue Potter still hadn't had that baby. It was more than a week overdue now and what would Sam do if …? Asa Morgan, the little boy Sam'd treated for poison ivy on Friday had come back Monday. He'd kept scratching it and now had a yellow pus-y infection on his calf. There'd been gashed fingers and kids with ear infections along with gall bladder attacks and kidney stones — which Sam couldn't do anything about but people came in for help anyway.

At least they did at first. But the numbers had tapered off — dramatically. Sam wanted to believe, *said* she believed, that was because folks were concerned about using up what little gasoline they had left, were taking care of their own issues at home.

She did *not* want to believe that fewer people used the clinic now because there were fewer people to need it. Fewer people period.

People vanishing.

"Is it just because everybody's scared, is that it?" Charlie said and Sam drew her thoughts back away from the abyss. "Is that what all the … violence is about?"

Sam didn't know where Charlie was going with the remark.

"I mean everybody cooped up together like this, a pressure cooker. Is that why … how many violent deaths have there been, in just this two-week period?"

There'd been Martha Whittiker. Somebody'd bashed in her head and then dumped her body in her grandson's apartment to blame it on him. That's what Liam thought, anyway. But Liam was murdered before he could prove it. And there was no doubt in Sam's mind who had shot him down in cold blood. The same person who'd hanged Dylan Shaw the next day when she had no proof he'd committed a crime. Viola Tackett wanted to demonstrate her authority and Dylan was the sacrificial goat on the altar of her dreams of conquest.

Howie Witherspoon had killed his wife and tried to kill his son, would have if Malachi hadn't stopped him. Shot him. And now Hayley Norman.

"Half a dozen people — Nower County's a more dangerous place than the east side of Chicago!" When

Charlie spoke again, the bravado had drained out of her voice. "And when Viola Tackett finds out Malachi didn't stand down like she told him to … we'll be adding my name to the list of—"

"That's not going to happen!" Sam hoped there was more confidence in her voice than she felt. In truth, she was terrified that at any minute Viola Tackett would come charging into her house — where Charlie was staying — with guns blazing. "We're going to figure this out. We're going to get out of here!"

She saw Charlie look at her watch and shake her head. Maybe Charlie had noticed the same thing Sam had noticed, but Sam didn't ask … because she flat-out didn't want to know. She didn't want to be right … that time was no longer moving too fast in the world of the Jabberwock. Now, it was moving too slow.

Chapter Twenty-Two

Douglas screamed. Shrieked. The cry didn't even sound human, a screeching wail that cored its way into Rusty's soul. The sound became a permanent part of Rusty in that frozen moment and he'd remember the sound for the rest of his life.

Rusty knew what happened even before he turned around because he had heard the rattle, but maybe Douglas never did. It was impossible to find out what Douglas had or hadn't heard or seen or felt because the moment the rattlesnake sunk in its fangs, Douglas Taylor left the building. He was never again coherent. He was either screaming or hysterical or … but that part was later.

"Douglas." The name rode the breath knocked out of Rusty's lungs, whispered because there was not enough air to say the word out loud.

Douglas was writhing on his back in the leaves, kicking his feet like he was throwing a tantrum, and holding his left hand with his right. The left was already beginning to swell. He had his head tilted back and the veins in his neck bulged as he shrieked.

All that was a horrifying sight. But more horrifying by far was the sight of the rattlesnake that had bitten him. It lay in the dirt only a couple of feet from Douglas's face.

Rusty knew quite a bit about snakes, actually, had done a diorama of a snake's habitat in fourth grade. The snake he had used as an example looked just like this one — greenish brown with gray V-shaped bands evenly spaced along its body. A timber rattlesnake.

The one that lay in the dried leaves beside a shrieking Douglas was huge, maybe four feet long, and it seemed to Rusty that the sound of its rattle was even louder than Douglas's screams.

Words formed in Rusty's frozen mind like the answers to questions on a Magic 8-Ball. Just suddenly there out of the dark water. The words were the first line of the report he'd turned in with the idiot diorama — "The most important thing to do if you find a rattlesnake in the woods is to get away from it, moving slowly backwards. If threatened, rattlesnakes can and often do strike more than one time, and the snake determines the amount of venom to inject with each bite."

Rusty grabbed hold of Douglas's flailing foot and began dragging him down the steep slope away from the snake. He was hard to hold onto because he was wiggling and squirming and screaming, but downhill helped. The big timber rattler made no move in their direction. It slithered away into the dead leaves and its camouflage quickly made it invisible but Rusty kept an iron grip on Douglas's ankle until he'd dragged the boy thirty or forty feet away from where the snake had struck. Then he let go of the boy's foot and dropped to his knees beside Douglas, crying out his name even though he knew Douglas couldn't hear him.

Douglas's left hand was swelling and turning purple —

you could actually *watch* it getting bigger and bigger. The boy's face was pale and he had broken out into a full body sweat.

The weight of responsibility landed on Rusty with the force of a piano thrown out a third-floor window onto his head.

He had to do something. He had to do the *right* something. And he had to do it *fast.*

And he was so scared. Not one time in the entire twelve years that Rusty Sheridan had been drawing regular breaths on the earth had he ever been this terrified.

If he didn't do the right thing, or did something and it was wrong, Douglas could … He wouldn't let his mind go any further than that, but the sight of the swelling hand *and wrist* made a statement that didn't need words.

Think. *Think!*

He tried, but his thoughts were spinning around and around in his head and he only seemed able to hold onto one of them long enough to think a little piece of it before another shoved it out of place and demanded he attend to it.

… raise the area above the level of the heart …

… cut the wound … no, don't cut the wound …

… suck out the venom … no, that'll only …

Use a tourniquet.

Apply ice.

Then Rusty screamed, a cry wild and Jurassic in its fury and fear, seared his throat as he roared out of him, ripped out his chest.

He screamed and screamed.

Let his voice mingle with Douglas's in a duet of terror and pain and fear.

And then he didn't scream. He cut off in mid-cry.

Douglas never stopped screaming, but he wasn't as

loud as before, perhaps because he was getting hoarse. Or perhaps because he couldn't catch his breath.

Rusty's screams stopped because his thoughts had finally ordered themselves. One big thought had stopped in its tracks and all the little spinning ones had crashed into the back of it.

I have to get help.

Other reasonable instructions followed in the wake of the big thought, but the imperative *"Get Help"* was lit up like a flashing neon sign in his brain.

Keep him still.

Let the wound bleed … some of the venom will be washed out by the blood. But Douglas's bite, two ugly black holes on the back of his hand, was not bleeding. Likely because blood flow had been cut off by the swelling. His hand was already almost twice normal size in just …

How long?

How long ago was he bitten?

That seemed like a piece of information Rusty needed to know, but he didn't wear a watch and had no idea.

Keep him still. Keep him quiet. Keep him calm.

Negatory to all of the above. The only possible course of action Rusty could see lay in two opposite directions.

He could leave Douglas here and go for help. Or he could try to get Douglas out of the woods by himself.

He probably should have chosen Door A. It was probably the smartest course of action, but he could not make himself do it. He could not make himself leave a ten-year-old boy whose hand and arm were swollen and purple, lying on the ground screaming.

And what if he couldn't find where he'd left him?

These weren't woods Rusty was familiar with. He knew the way back to Douglas's house, but there was no guarantee he would be able to retrace his steps back to this particular spot in the woods.

He had to get Douglas out.

How?

Carry him?

Rusty was his mother's son, tall and lanky … and slender. Douglas was his physical opposite. And the way back to Douglas's house was up and over Donavon Rock. They'd crossed the big outcrop on the way here. It was the boundary beyond which Douglas's mother absolutely forbid him to play. Because in the opposite direction, downhill, was the Beaufort County line.

Rusty scooped Douglas into his arms, the way the hero always carried the frightened woman out of the burning building. He made it maybe a dozen steps before he had to go down on his knees and dump Douglas out onto the ground.

Holding Douglas was like holding a fish on the end of a line, flipping and flopping around. He was still kicking his feet, but not as hard, and the swelling from the bite had now spread beyond his wrist and into his forearm. He was still screaming, but that had become ragged and sporadic. Rusty could hear him struggling to draw in enough air to scream.

Over his shoulder, then. He muscled Douglas's wiggling body up onto his shoulder, held onto his right leg and arm and staggered a few steps uphill. Once he got to the top of the ridge, he prayed he'd be able to see Douglas's house. But even if he couldn't, he could go down the other side of the ridge and he'd eventually come out on Bethel Park Pike where he could flag somebody down.

Rusty tried.

He had never in his life tried any harder to do a thing than he tried to carry Douglas, but he flat-out wasn't strong enough. Even using his legs to lift and holding Douglas's weight with his whole body and not just his arms he made it maybe fifty yards and his knees fell out from under him and both of them tumbled to the ground.

Rusty rolled Douglas over onto his back, kneeling beside him and got a good look at his arm and hand. The swelling had reached the elbow. The hand was turning from fiery red to a deep, ugly shade of purple.

Rusty burst out sobbing, rocking back and forth on his knees, crying like a little baby.

The words from the report he'd written for the fourth-grade diorama floated up into the eight-ball window in his mind.

"Rattlesnake bites are rarely fatal in a healthy adult with proper medical care. If antivenin treatment is given within two hours after the bite, the probability of recovery is greater than ninety-nine percent."

He tried not to see the remainder of the words on the white thing floating in the black eight-ball water. "Left untreated, a bite can cause internal hemorrhaging leading to death."

Staggering to his feet, he picked up Douglas's foot and started to drag him, knew it was futile but did it anyway. Douglas was too heavy and the ridge incline was too steep. Maybe if it was downhill. But downhill was the county line.

And the Jabberwock.

Chapter Twenty-Three

Downhill was the Jabberwock.

A horrifying plan began to form in Rusty's mind. Actually, it had been forming for some time, but he had managed to ignore it until now. But as he dug his shoes into the loose soil and dead leaves of the slope and pulled with all his might to drag Douglas along behind him, the thought stepped out into centerstage in his mind.

It stood there, hot and stinking and demanded to be heard.

Downhill was the county line.

Downhill was the Jabberwock.

… and what happened when you crossed the Jabberwock?

You were suddenly sitting in the Dollar Store parking lot in the Middle of Nowhere desperately sick.

In the Middle of Nowhere.

The geographic center of Nowhere County was a far better place for Douglas to be right now than in the woods on the far side of Donavon Rock in Freeman Hollow.

If Rusty carried Douglas into the Jabberwock …

But they would be sick. Horribly, desperately sick. Everyone who'd ever dared cross the Jabberwock said the experience was one of the worst things they'd ever gone through.

Yeah, it'd be awful.

But as far as Rusty knew, Jabberwock sickness had never *killed* anybody. Correction, Willie Cochran, that old guy from Wiley who didn't have thumbs, had died after coming through, but Rusty's mom said he'd had a bad heart that couldn't stand the strain.

Well, Douglas had a rattlesnake bite. His whole arm was turning purple. Could *he* stand the strain? In his condition, would the Jabberwock kill him?

Rusty dropped Douglas's foot into the dry leaves and stood very still, looking back down the hillside. From here it wasn't visible, but it probably wasn't more than a couple of hundred yards to the shimmering mirage in the trees that marked the domain of the dragon.

His mother had taken him with her out to the county line to show it to him, to a remote spot, on the other side of the one-lane covered bridge on Wiley Road. That was one of the multitude of things Rusty loved about his mother. She took him to see the Jabberwock, knew he'd be curious, thought he had a right to see it for himself. Other boys he knew weren't so fortunate. Their parents — their mothers, they all came from "adult-male free" homes, which Rusty saw as infinitely preferable to being yo-yoed into and out of the lives of a string of men like Douglas was. His mother called it "sequential polygamy" and she thought he knew what that meant so he'd never asked.

The day she took him to the county line on Wiley Road, his mom had walked with him slowly toward their mirror images in the wiggly shimmer in the road. She'd told him about how she had touched her hand to her own image, and described in gory detail what that had cost her. She'd pointed out to him what the Jabberwock looked like in the meadow beside the road, how it made the grass blurry where it touched the ground, and she'd shown him the sparkling spiderweb quality of the Jabberwock in the woods.

That was the first but not the last time Rusty had seen it, though it was the first time he'd been out in the open where he could see his reflection in it. He was sure he could find it now in the trees at the bottom of the hill.

What should he do? What did he dare do?

He could keep struggling to carry/drag Douglas up the ridge, over Donavon Rock and back down the other side. In brutal honesty, that was futile. He could leave Douglas here, mark the spot somehow so he could find it again, and race off for help. And leave Douglas here in the woods alone.

Or he could drag Douglas downhill to the Jabberwock, and let the Jabberwock do the transporting.

It had a big price tag, but it seemed the only viable option. It would make Douglas desperately sick. It would make *Rusty* desperately sick, too. *Please, a nosebleed — even if I bleed to death. Or blind. Not puking.*

"He'll die if I don't get this right." Rusty said the words aloud, sobbed them out into the forest that was now mostly quiet. Douglas wasn't screaming anymore.

If the Jabberwock killed Douglas, it would be Rusty's fault for taking him there. If he died of the snakebite after Rusty had struggled for hours to get help for him ... well, that was just too bad. Rusty'd done all he could.

But he wouldn't let himself look at it that way. His mother had taught him better than that. This wasn't about Rusty right now, about how he'd be judged someday. It was about Douglas, a life and death decision. What might happen to Rusty because of his decision wasn't the point and he wasn't allowed to let it influence what he decided.

He thought he saw a sparkle, a twinkle in the trees. Maybe it was closer than he thought. He patted Douglas's shirt pocket. Douglas always carried a pen in his shirt pocket. Rusty should have told him a long time ago that it made him look like a nerd, but he hadn't wanted to hurt Douglas's feelings. Rusty used the pen to write on Douglas's pasty white forehead "Rattlesnake bite" because he was afraid he might be too sick to tell them what was wrong with Douglas at the other end.

And then he turned around, grabbed Douglas under both arms, and began hauling him down the hillside, his heels making twin grooves like railroad tracks in the dirt.

Chapter Twenty-Four

Duncan Norman couldn't breathe.

The words screamed at him, leapt up off the page and attracted his very soul. His hands began to shake so violently he dropped the book into his lap, but he instantly snatched it back up and held it to his chest, hugged it to his chest, held on with the kind of fierce tenderness he would have held his precious Hayley if she had told him what happened.

Dear God in heaven, his precious child had been raped.

Raped!

He couldn't stand the knowledge. Reading the journal had been a ride through the hells of adolescence. Pain and humiliation were recorded in detail on page after page. The fat girl. Hayley Whaley. It wasn't a diary, a record of events and activities. It was a place where Hayley poured out her soul. The entries weren't dated. Each new one started a fresh page, and rambled on. The final entry in the journal had been a description of the act that would lead her to her death.

Duncan couldn't stand the images the words drew in his mind, wanted to leap out of his skin with rage and horror. It was worse than knowing she was dead. Knowing she had been used that way, was worse than …

The thought had been swirling around with all the others in his head, a cacophony of confusion, but it suddenly stepped out onto centerstage, stood in the spotlight and demanded to be heard.

That's *why* she was dead!

Because she had been raped. She had been deflowered, had lost her virginity in a brutal act too horrific to contemplate. And it had shattered her, broken her. His sweet, precious baby … she couldn't stand to live with the degradation. That's *why!* That's why she had killed herself, to escape the horror.

He sucked in a sob, still clutching the book to his chest, the waves of horror and revulsion and grief slamming into him like breakers on the rocks.

"Duncan …"

It was Miriam, at the door. She had probably knocked but he hadn't heard her. "Norman … please, honey. Come out, don't stay locked up in there in Hayley's room."

Miriam must never know. She must never find out that her baby girl had been ravaged by a monster and had been so devastated by the attack that she didn't want to live anymore. No one must know.

Precious Hayley had kept her secret, took it with her to the grave and he would honor that.

If someone *knew* … that would be the end. The end of everything.

"Not now," he said, marveling that his mind could formulate words and his mouth articulate them, his throat form the sound to carry them forward.

Duncan Norman had always been a private man.

Suited more for study and contemplation than for the more hands-on part of ministry. In truth, he often wondered if it would have been better if he'd become a priest instead of a Pentecostal minister. Of course, that was out of the question. Priests were Cath-o-liks, they worshiped idols, statues of Jesus and his mother. They would burn in hell, every last one of them.

But the priesthood, as Duncan understood it, held an enormous appeal. He would have been a monk, of course, like the ones at the monastery in Gethsemane in Marion County. A life of solitude and study, of denial of self, of contemplation and service. A life where he did not have to deal with the ugliness of life in the world God had given over to Satan, the prince of this world, for a time.

The ugliness of sin in all its various forms and manifestations disgusted him. One reason he was so very stern, held onto himself so tightly, was because his whole body went into gritting-his-teeth mode when he was confronted with adultery and lying, stealing, fornication ... The list went on and on. And if Duncan had been a priest, he would have been above such things.

But he'd chosen ministry, and did his best to give of his limited amount of human compassion freely to the members of his congregation and to his family. It had taken a toll on him, but he had soldiered on, aiming for the prize, waiting for the crown of glory on the other side.

If he shared with Miriam the horror of what he had discovered, the awful knowledge would flow right out through her to every person she came in contact with. Miriam had no filters, nothing held back the revelation of her every thought and feeling. She would exude the knowledge of Hayley's humiliation, it would become a dark pall hanging over her as thick and putrid as stink rising up off roadkill.

Hayley deserved better than that. Her memory deserved better. He would keep the awful knowledge from Miriam to protect the honor of his child.

Except that's not why.

The why was that Duncan himself couldn't stand for the world to know. He couldn't stand the knowing looks, the sympathy, the understanding of all the whispered conversations that would go on all over the county, centered on her precious child and how she had lost her virginity to a—

All his spinning thoughts stopped at the word.

Rapist.

Like the train cars behind a stalled engine, all his thoughts slammed into that one and then fell over onto their sides, unable to move forwards.

Who?

Who had done such a thing?

Who had raped …

He opened the book he had clutched to his chest and re-read the entry.

A man had found Hayley at the Scott's Ridge overlook alone. She often went there to be by herself. Duncan knew that but it never occurred to him she wasn't safe there or he never would have allowed …

No, he would not assume the tiniest portion of the blame for the horror that had befallen his little girl. All the blame for that belonged to the man who had violated her.

Hayley described him as tall and dark. Said he had a rugged face, unruly black hair and piercing blue eyes.

An oddly detailed description of the man she saw through tears after he had ripped her clothes off, threw her onto her back on the picnic table and had his way with her.

When had it happened? How long had the poor child

been carrying this burden alone? He understood why she hadn't told him. How could a teenage girl tell her father a thing like that? She had been brave, kept her pain and humiliation to herself until …

Until what?

What had triggered the final desolation so complete she couldn't stand the thought of life after it? Why had—?

A thought so monstrous it made Duncan nauseous, crawled into his belly and began to gnaw at his guts, a lazy rat of horror.

What if …

What if … Hayley had been … *pregnant?*

No. Absolutely not.

The blows falling on him one after another left him reeling. He had stood up at some point, holding the book, clutching it to his chest, and he realized that now he was perched on the little pink stool in front of Hayley's dressing table, where she sat to put on her makeup and curl her hair.

He glanced into the mirror and saw how foolish he looked, a man in a dark suit — he always wore dark suits and white shirts. Other ministers he knew had given in to wearing pastel colors, what was it they called it — French blue. But not Duncan. Duncan …

Pregnant!

The word reverberated in his head, sounded like the resounding beat of a kettle drum between his ears.

Surely, not … Why would he think such a thing? That was ridiculous. What—?

Where had Hayley been going on J-Day? It was such an odd thing to do, something she had never done before. She had waited until he left for the church and then had taken her mother's car … where? Where was she going when she hit the Jabberwock?

Was she going to a clinic … somewhere to find out if she was pregnant?

Or … oh, dear God— No.

He couldn't stand this, couldn't stand where his mind was taking him, leapt up off the stool and began to pace back and forth across the room, up onto the Little Mermaid rug Miriam'd insisted they give Hayley for Christmas, the one she'd pretended to like but didn't really. He knew Hayley thought it was too "little girl," and she was right. It was. Miriam never wanted "her baby" to grow up. Now, she never would.

Back and forth.

Back and forth.

Abortion.

It made sense.

It all made sense.

Hayley had been raped. She had conceived. And she had … been planning to get an abortion when the Jabberwock threw her into the Middle of Nowhere.

And that's why she had killed herself. When she realized she couldn't leave the county, couldn't get out to … she was carrying the child of a rapist.

A rapist.

Of course, she had seen no other out than suicide.

There was another knock at the door. This time it wasn't timid, it was assertive.

"Pastor Norman, it's me, Joe. Can I come in? Or would you come out? You hadn't ought to be alone right now. Can we pray together?"

Duncan opened the door, but instead of inviting Joe in, Duncan held out his hand.

"Can I have the keys to your car? I need to borrow it for a while."

The Jabberwock had eaten one of their cars and

Hayley had used the other to go … to the Scott's Ridge Overlook. That's where the car was. She had parked it in the lot there, walked to the ledge, and leapt off.

"What … where do you need to—?"

"Out. I have somewhere I have to go, someone I have to see."

"I'll go with you, drive you. You don't need to be driving—"

Duncan brushed past him and strode down the hallway, took the stairs two at a time and approached the first person he saw — Mamie Butterfield, who was standing in the doorway to the parlor.

"Mamie, I need to borrow your car."

"Why sure … what do you need the car for, Pastor Norman?"

"Please don't ask right now. I can't … I have to see someone. Please."

Mamie was constantly losing things, so she wore her purse on a strap around her shoulder to keep up with it. She dug around inside it for a moment and then brought out a set of keys. The keys dangled from a keyring with a Papa Smurf fob.

Miriam saw him heading for the front door and called out to him, but he only tossed a "I have to go somewhere" over his shoulder and continued to Mamie Butterfield's old Pontiac parked out front. When he closed the door, he saw that several people had followed him out of the house and were standing on the porch watching him. With great effort, he managed the self-control to pull slowly out of the space in front of his house and drive cautiously down the street. As soon as he was out of sight of the house, he gunned it, driving so fast he could barely keep the car on the road.

He was on his way to the Middle of Nowhere. Sam

Sheridan would be there and if she wasn't they'd know where he could find her. He had to talk to her, ask her what she knew, because she was the one person Hayley might have confided in. And Duncan had to find out if his little girl was carrying the baby of a rapist when she threw herself off the top of the ridge.

He had to know.

Chapter Twenty-Five

THE WORLD HAD TAKEN on a kind of surreal glow by the time Sam and Charlie got back to the veterinary clinic from Persimmon Ridge, where Sam had told the Normans their only child was dead.

It seemed to take forever to get to the Middle of Nowhere, like the drive was thirty miles instead of six.

Thelma Jackson was gone. Though Sam still had questions for her, she was glad she didn't have to ask them right now because her mind felt like it was wrapped in cotton. Charlie took Merrie back to Sam's to get a quick lunch and a "mini-nap" before her shift with E.J. Sam just ... went on autopilot. She went into the building, donned her white yep-I'm-a-doctor-alright lab coat, checked on E.J., under the watchful eye of Doreen Jaggers, and surveyed the empty waiting room, profoundly grateful there were no patients waiting.

When she went into the breakroom, she was surprised to find Malachi, sipping a cup of road tar. She was sure he'd ask how it had gone with the Normans, which she didn't want to talk about, and then he'd want to discuss what Thelma'd told them. And she didn't want to talk about that either.

She sat down but was spared both discussions.

Pete Rutherford didn't knock on the door, he just burst into the room.

"Sam, you got to come quick. It's bad."

An incoming, of course. Someone had either accidentally or purposefully challenged the Jabberwock and was now out there in the parking lot paying the price for that mistake. And they all were bad.

Pete hung there for another beat. There was more.

"It's two kids. And one of 'em's Rusty."

That was absurd, of course. Pete was mistaken.

Sam thought that thought and fifty more of them in the second it took her to rise out of her seat.

It couldn't be Rusty. Rusty was on the other side of Twig, spending the afternoon with his friend Douglas Taylor.

And Rusty wouldn't run afoul of the Jabberwock. Sam had made sure he wouldn't. She knew enough about kids in general and her son in particular to know that once news about the Jabberwock got out, he would be filled to bursting with curiosity about the it. Duh. Of course he would. He was resourceful enough to find some way to satisfy his curiosity. Better that she be there when he did. Because twelve-year-old boys were invincible, they were bulletproof, they were going to live a thousand years. Danger? Pffffft. Never gave it a thought, or if they did, they certainly didn't let on that they did.

So she took Rusty out to the other side of the North Fork River on Wiley Road to the county line and showed him the Jabberwock, told him about her ride on the beast, from the Danville Pike county border with Beaufort County to the Middle of Nowhere. And, gross as it was, she had taken him with her to the Middle of Nowhere and let him see for himself what happened to the people who tangled with the beast. Sam also told Rusty in brutal detail what had happened to Abby Clayton.

No way would that kid have gone through the Jabberwock. No way.

She kept telling herself that as she ran out the door and across the parking lot to the bus shelter. That's where she stopped telling herself, when she saw the unmistakable reddish-brown hair on the young boy who was vomiting so violently he was spraying blood out his nose.

But it was the boy beside him that stopped Sam in her tracks. Printed on his forehead were the words: rattlesnake bite. Not that she'd needed an explanation.

Rusty saw her then, or at least became aware of her presence and managed to force words through and around the heaving.

"Big one. Timber rattler."

The boy was Douglas Taylor and he was, indeed, in bad shape. His whole left arm was swollen to twice its size, all the way to the shoulder. His hand had turned an angry purple color, with two oozing indentions on the back of it. And he was bleeding. His nose was an open spigot of blood that would have drowned him if Pete hadn't had the presence of mind to roll him onto his side. The nosebleed was courtesy of the Jabberwock. Everything else was courtesy of a timber rattlesnake.

She knelt and took hold of the wrist on his right hand. His pulse was rapid and thready, his face as white as a sack of flour, he was sweating and gasping for breath.

She looked up at Pete, who had come back out behind

her. He knelt on the ground on the other side of Douglas, while she heard Rusty heaving and heaving behind her. She looked into Pete's eyes.

"Do you have any—?" he asked.

"Antivenom? No."

The survival rate for rattlesnake bites was higher than ninety percent — *if* the victim received antivenin within two hours after the bite. Sam didn't know how much time had elapsed since Douglas had been bitten, but it hardly mattered. Without the antivenin, there was really nothing she could do.

"How did he end up in the Jabberwock?" Pete asked and Sam instantly understood. She turned toward Rusty and froze in place like a statue. Malachi had come out of the building behind her and Pete. He had apparently lifted/helped Rusty up onto the bus shelter bench and was sitting beside the boy, holding his head as he heaved.

Malachi saw her staring, misread the stunned look on her face.

"He's fine," he said, then nodded toward Douglas. "Wrote rattlesnake bite on his forehead because he knew somebody on the other end would need to know that. He did it on purpose, rode the Jabberwock to get his friend help."

Malachi was right of, course. Rusty had gone through all that ... and it didn't matter. If Sam had been standing beside Douglas when he got bit she could have done no more for him than she could right now.

Without antivenom ... there wasn't a thing she could do to save the boy's life. And from the look of him, it wasn't likely to last much longer.

"Call his mother," Sam instructed Raylynn, who stood beside where Pete knelt. "Her name's Claire ... not Taylor

… McFarland. If you can't find that number, call Little Elmer Jones. He lives down the road, so do the Callaways. She needs to get here as fast as she can.

What she didn't say was, "so she can say goodbye to her son."

Chapter Twenty-Six

DUNCAN NORMAN HAD NEVER BEEN in more of a hurry in his life, never been driven by such a need in his life, but when he arrived in Mamie Butterfield's car at the parking lot of the Dollar General Store in the Middle of Nowhere, the pandemonium he found there stopped him in his tracks.

Standing on the outside of the crowd gathered there, he grasped quickly that somebody had ridden the Jabber-wock, as the kids called it, to the parking lot and that the crowd had gathered to care for them. But it was much bigger than that, as he found out when a second car careened into the parking lot minutes after his did and a woman leapt out of the passenger side door and raced to the spot where the caregivers were crowded around a body on the asphalt.

It was Claire Taylor. But that wasn't her name now, he didn't think. She and her little boy, Douglas, had come to Duncan's church a time or two before she had married the last of … he didn't know how many husbands. This one, whose last name was McArthur or McFarland, something like that, didn't have any use for "religion."

The hysterical scene that played out then as Duncan watched should have broken his heart. It didn't. His pastor's heart should have ached with compassion for the poor woman whose son had been bitten by a rattlesnake. He should have *cared*. But he discovered to his dismay that he had no caring left inside. He was a hollow man, his chest as empty as the Tin Man in *The Wizard of Oz*. Every feeling, every emotion he possessed, had died with his little girl.

He'd heard the grieving say things like that, but he had never before understood what they meant. Now, he knew that everything a parent was, all the emotional investment, the care, the love, the faith and hope they had invested in their child, vanished when the child died. And that left the parents with only a vacuum in their chests. Hollow and unable to give anything to anybody because they had not even sufficient emotional resources for themselves.

For the first time in … since he had entered the ministry, Duncan Norman was a spectator to human tragedy, an onlooker. Not a participant, not engaged in an effort to heal the grief. Just there, watching. And in truth, he just wanted the whole thing to be over, for Claire to summon sufficient emotional control — not likely — or for somebody else to take charge of her. He needed for her drama to be over. He needed desperately to talk to Sam Sheridan.

SAM WOULD HAVE SWORN that it was impossible to feel any more helpless than she had felt when Judd Perkins hauled

E.J.'s body into the clinic, his leg a gory mess. He'd been in agony and Sam couldn't even ease his pain! Until she could. Malachi had provided a bottle of oxycontin. Sam didn't even know how many pills were in the bottle but it didn't matter because Malachi had a limitless supply.

But Malachi had no magic pills to relieve the suffering of the little boy who lay before her now. There was at least hope for E.J. Maybe they would be able to do something before it was too late. And they had time to try. At least *try*.

This little boy had no hope. It was already too late. A small boy and a *big* snake — she could tell it was huge by the size of the puncture wounds and the distance they were apart. Given the speed and amount of the swelling, the snake had injected a full load of venom into the bite. It would have been touch-and-go even if Sam'd been right there with a syringe full of antivenin and a cotton ball already dabbed in alcohol.

This little boy was going to die. Rusty's friend. A friend her son had been willing to challenge the horror of the Jabberwock to save. She was so proud of Rusty.

It seemed to Sam that time turned into molasses — on a cold winter morning. It oozed by thick and slow. Every second took an hour to pass and during that hour Douglas's symptoms worsened.

The boy would not last long in his condition. His breathing was labored and ragged, his heartbeat the flutter of a hummingbird's wings. The exact nature of how he would die wasn't yet apparent. He was in shock and severe shock could shut down the heart or lead to a catastrophic stroke. But if Sam had to guess, she thought it would be a sudden cascading of organ failures, one leading to another until his heart … just stopped.

Where was—?

A car careened into the parking lot of the Dollar General Store, and before it came to a complete stop, out leapt a woman with flaming red hair — a Sears color. She looked around frantically, spotted the clot of people clustered around the bus shelter and raced toward them, likely unaware that she had lost a shoe somewhere, and was proceeding aboard a lone flip-flop that came off before she reached them.

She saw the boy lying on the asphalt and screamed.

It was a horrifying sound, a primal, almost feral sound that made the small hairs on the back of Sam's neck stand on end.

Dropping to her knees beside Douglas, she looked pleadingly at Sam.

Her words came out in a single hysterical babble, with pauses only when she ran out of breath.

"Is he alright, tell me he's alright, that he's going to be alright, dear sweet Jesus God look at his arm. You have to do something, give him something, fix that poor swollen arm. Dougie, Mommy's here. Can you hear me? Open your eyes, sweet baby, and talk to me, tell me you're going to be okay. Don't just lay there like that, talk to me. Dougie, you're scaring Mommy. Talk to me."

When she paused for a breath, Sam put in as kindly as she could.

"He can't speak right now, Mrs. McFarland. He's unconscious. But he can hear. Talk to him. He can hear you."

Mrs. McFarland leaned over her son and began to shout. Sam hadn't said that it was hard for Douglas to hear but his mother must have taken it that way because she spoke to him like he was behind a closed door.

"Dougie! Dougie, I'm here, Mommy's here. You're

going to be fine, just fine. You got bit by a rattlesnake but it was a little bitty one, not big around as a pencil. Didn't have hardly no venom at all. Dougie, can you hear me?"

She took his hand in hers, the hand not swollen to roughly the size of a catcher's mit.

"Squeeze my hand if you can hear me, okay? Come on, squeeze my hand."

Apparently, she felt nothing because she then instructed him to blink his eyes if he could hear her, but there was no response.

Finally, Claire recovered enough of her reason to want to know what her Dougie was doing out here in the parking lot, why whoever brought him here had left him outside instead of taking him into the veterinary clinic for treatment.

"Nobody brought him," Sam said. "He rode the Jabberwock."

For some reason those words hit Claire McFarland like a drop of water in hot grease.

"*Oh, no he didn't!* He couldn't have. Why, the county line is more than two miles from our house and he wasn't even in that part of the woods." She looked at him, her eyes caressing his face. "And he wouldn't have. I have told him about it. He knows to stay away. He couldn't have."

"Rusty used the Jabberwock to bring Douglas here after he was bitten," Sam said, and the woman's eyes snapped to her so fast there was almost an audible clacking in the sockets.

"Rusty took my Douglas into the Jabberwock?" She screamed the words.

"To get help for him. They were out in the woods and he—"

"If Douglas got bit by a snake, Rusty should have come

and gotten me. They were only a little way from the house."

She actually turned to Rusty then, who was totally unaware of her presence and didn't respond, probably didn't hear what she said to him.

"Rusty Sheridan, why didn't you come get me?"

"If they was close enough to the county line to cross it, they couldn't a'been playing in the woods next to your house," Pete said kindly, trying to reason with the woman.

"You don't know that. You don't know anything. Dougie is an obedient boy and I told him he couldn't go anywhere beyond sight of the house. He would never have disobeyed me. *Never!*"

She was still yelling now, probably didn't know it or what she was saying but her voice stopped in mid-cry when Douglas made an odd sound.

A rattling, choking sound replaced his labored breaths. His body lurched upward as if he were having a seizure, and maybe he was, and then he collapsed to the asphalt and lay still.

"Dougie …?"

His mother had a look of such shocked denial on her face, Sam suspected she genuinely didn't know that her little boy had just died. But Sam was wrong.

"Dougie!" she shrieked, wailed. She leaned over and pulled the child's body up into her arms as she shrieked, made sounds a human voice couldn't make as she held the boy and rocked his limp body back and forth.

"Nooooo!" She looked at Sam, pleading.

Someone knelt beside her, a man who must be her current husband. Sam had never met him.

He put his arm around her shoulders and said in a calm, quiet voice, "You got to lay him back now, Claire, let them folks see to him and tend to that bite. Put him down."

She bought instantly into the fantasy.

"You'll fix it, won't you, Sam? You'll make my Dougie better." She looked into her husband's eyes without seeing him. "He'll be fine. Just needs to rest, that's all. That bite is going to sting, though, when he wakes up. We need to stop by and make sure we got baby aspirin 'cause I bet I'm going to be up all night, rocking him."

Sam looked over Claire's head and made eye contact with her husband. "Why don't you take Claire inside, into the waiting room, while I … take care of Douglas." The man nodded.

Sam looked up at Malachi, who was no longer holding Rusty's head because the boy had finally stopped heaving, just sat with his head in his hands as if it felt fragile. Reaching into the pocket of her smock, she pulled out the bottle of oxycontin. It was neither a sedative nor a tranquilizer. Sam had none of either. Oxycontin was not designed to … but it would relax Claire, wrap her mind in a narcotic haze. It was all Sam had.

She opened the bottle, poured out a small handful of pills and gave them to the man kneeled beside Claire. "These will … help. No more than two every four hours. Let's get her inside, get her some water for the pills."

Claire allowed herself to be helped to her feet, turned and walked slowly between her husband and Malachi toward the animal hospital doorway.

Sam looked at Pete Rutherford, who seemed about to cry. She was glad Charlie wasn't here. Charlie knew what it felt like to lose a child.

At that moment, the fragile pink bubble of unreality that incased Claire McFarland burst. She stopped in her tracks, whirled around and raced back across the parking lot.

Not to the spot where Douglas lay dead on the asphalt. She ran to Rusty.

"What did you *do?*" she screamed at the boy. Rusty lifted his head when she spoke, with the pinched look on his face that told Sam he had a needle in his brain like Liam Montgomery'd had when he showed up in the Middle of Nowhere.

Rusty didn't try to answer, probably couldn't talk and certainly didn't know what to say if he could.

"Why did you drag my baby off to play in the woods where he didn't want to go?"

She didn't give him a chance to reply, even if he'd been able.

"Why didn't you help him? Why didn't you come get me? Why didn't you *carry him home* to his mommy?"

"We were so far—" The words were a ragged whisper.

"So far? *Far?* My Dougie wouldn't have gone so far if you hadn't made him. He trusted you, looked up to you. He would have done anything you told him."

Sam didn't know when she had crossed the space between them, only knew that she had shoved her way in front of Rusty.

"Rusty did the best he could." Sam's husky voice was an octave lower, in a tone that would brook no argument. "Douglas is too big to carry—"

The woman turned on Sam with the speed of a striking snake.

"My Dougie is *not fat!* He's just a little boy, not heavy at all! Rusty was too lazy to pick him up and carry him so he pushed my poor little baby into the Jabberwock! Why …"

And then the light of reason blinked out in her eyes. Insanity fired there in its place, as bright as a road flare.

"*That's* what's wrong with my Dougie. Not some little snake bite. People get bit by snakes all the time, it's nothing.

It's the Jabberwock! Why Abby Clayton exploded when she—" She'd have lunged at Rusty if Sam hadn't been in her way. "And *you*! You pushed him into the Jabberwock. *You killed my precious baby!*"

And then Claire McFarland began to howl.

Chapter Twenty-Seven

IT SEEMED like an eternity before Duncan Norman was able to catch Sam Sheridan's eye. She was standing with a small group of people watching the pickup truck bearing the lifeless body of Douglas Taylor away. He thought maybe it was Pete Rutherford's truck, but he hadn't been paying that close attention. They had forced some kind of pills down Claire whatever-her-last-name-was-now and she'd finally stopped shrieking and zoned out enough for her husband to get her into the car and take her home.

As soon as Duncan got Sam's attention, her emotional withdrawal informed him instantly that she knew why he was here and that he wasn't going to like what she told him.

He approached her and asked softly, "May I please have a moment, Miss Sheridan?"

She said nothing, just nodded and led him away from the crowd to a quiet spot beneath the awning that stretched out over the front of the veterinary clinic.

No sense mincing words.

"Do you know if ... was my daughter ... was Hayley

pregnant?" The last word came out in a strangled sob, tangled with such horror it was barely able to escape from his throat at all.

"Yes." She just looked at him then, like she was deciding how much more she should say.

"Please," and he heard the naked need in the word, the anguish he had only heard in the voices of others but had never expressed himself. "Don't hold back … tell me … the rest of it."

"On J-Day, she had been on her way to Lexington to … get an abortion."

He felt an involuntary spasm in his belly and was so suddenly nauseous he could only barely control it.

"Abortion." Even saying the word out loud refused to make it real.

"On Saturday afternoon, she asked me if I would do the procedure and I told her no."

A sob escaped then, a small one, like a sound a child would make.

"So she had no other choice …" He spoke the words as he thought them. "She saw no way out. When you wouldn't … she took her own life."

He stood, trying to absorb the meaning in his own words, almost missed what Sam said next.

"No, actually, she didn't."

"Didn't what?"

"Hayley didn't commit suicide."

"What are you saying? How could she … what, it was an *accident?* She … what, she tripped and fell to her death?"

"No, sir." He could tell she absolutely did not want to tell him any more, and he could feel the pressure of it. The horror of the unsaid. The monster evil growing bigger and bigger with every second of silence. "The fall off Scott's Ridge didn't kill her. She was already dead."

"Already dead?" That didn't make any sense.

"Reverend Norman, I don't know how to say this, but ... Hayley's death wasn't a suicide and it wasn't an accident. Hayley was murdered."

He thought she said murdered.

"What?"

"I'm no forensic pathologist, but ... there were wounds on the back of her head and on the front of her head. Wounds you don't get falling off a cliff."

"Wounds?" He was trying to track, but the meaning of her words seemed to be lagging behind the sound of them in his ears.

"Someone beat your daughter to death and then threw her body off the Scott's Ridge Overlook." The words came from behind him and he turned to see the woman — he couldn't think of her name — who had come with Sam earlier to deliver the news. She hadn't been here before. He didn't know when she'd arrived, but she was here now, standing beside a man, Viola's Tackett's son, Malachi.

"If Liam were here, he would have ... but he isn't," she said. Her name. He couldn't think of her name. "There's no one to conduct a ... murder investigation, but that's what it is. Hayley was murdered."

"But who—?" Then he knew, of course. There was only one explanation. The rapist who ravished his virginal daughter and planted his devil's seed in her womb had killed her to keep her silent.

"I'm sorry for your loss," said the man, Malachi. "If there's anything I can do ..." His voice trailed off.

Duncan looked at him then, really looked at him for the first time.

Malachi Tackett.

Malachi. Tackett.

Sam Sheridan was speaking but Duncan couldn't hear

her. There was a great roaring sound in his ears, the sound of all the engines in hell revving up like the tractors at the starting line at a tractor pull. The sound was deafening.

He was surprised he was able to speak, but found the words coming unbidden out past his lips. Looking the man full in the eye, Duncan said, "Actually, I could use your help. Clearly, my daughter drove out to the overlook, took our only car. Would you mind giving me a lift to go get it?"

His words had sounded as devoid of emotion as an automated attendant, as that voice in the airport that directs you to the right luggage carousel in baggage claim.

Everyone was surprised, of course. It was a totally off-the-wall request. Why ask someone you hardly knew to do a thing like that when there were a dozen people — church members and such — who'd jump at the chance to help out?

"I could ask … Scott's Ridge is where Hayley *died*. I'm not sure I'll be able to hold it together when I go there and I'd rather not fall apart in front of … someone from my church."

It wasn't a particularly good lie, but Duncan was mildly amused at how easily it had formed in his head. If he put his mind to it, he might be able to come up with a really good one. Effective lying likely took practice.

Then Duncan merely stood, looking at Malachi.

"Actually, I don't have a car myself …"

When Duncan didn't allow the explanation to get him off the hook, Malachi turned toward the woman — Charlie, her name was Charlie — and she took the non-verbal handoff.

"You're welcome to borrow mine."

"Thanks," he told her. Then he turned back to Duncan. "So when …?"

"Tomorrow morning," Duncan heard himself say. "I

have … things to attend to before … but I'll be free by nine o'clock. Could you pick me up at my house?"

"Sure," Malachi said.

A handshake was called for now and Duncan should have initiated it, should have said thank you as he … but he couldn't extend his hand. You could've put a gun to Duncan Norman's temple, cocked it, demanded that he shake Malachi Tackett's hand or you'd blow his brains out, and he'd have died right there on the spot.

He would not, he *could* not touch the man.

So Duncan merely turned on his heel and walked away. Had to walk away quickly, had to get away or he would …

The words Hayley had poured out into her diary spoke now in his head with her voice.

… *tall and dark with a rugged face, unruly black hair and piercing blue eyes.*

Malachi Tackett.

There was not another man in all of Nowhere County who fit that description so perfectly.

Malachi Tackett had raped and murdered his little girl. And Duncan Norman would assume the role of an avenging God, administering justice and retribution.

Tomorrow morning would give him enough time to lay his hands on a gun.

Chapter Twenty-Eight

RUSTY FELT his mother's hand on his shoulder, shaking him awake. He'd dozed off reading a comic book.

When he opened his eyes, it wasn't his mother standing in the room. It was Douglas Taylor's mother, Claire MacFarland.

"Get up," she told him. "You're coming with me."

"Huh?" He had to be dreaming. And it wasn't surprising that he was having a nightmare about Mrs. McFarland. He had never seen anything like the look in her eyes when she had screamed at him this afternoon. It was like … looking into the eyes of a mad dog. There was no reason there. He'd asked his mother later if the woman was insane and she'd said no but he didn't think she was right. He thought Mrs. McFarland had lost her mind.

The woman who was looking down at him now definitely looked crazy.

"Where's my mom?" he asked.

He knew where she was. She was *not* home. She was at the veterinary clinic in the Middle of Nowhere.

"You get up out of that bed, young man, or I will drag you out of it by your ear," Mrs. McFarland said. "Now!"

She had gone from zero to sixty in the yelling department in an instant.

"I … I got to get dressed."

"You think I ain't never seen a boy in his underwear. My Dougie …" She stopped, looked momentarily confused. Rusty was seized by the urge to shove her out of the way and bolt out of the room. He was sure he could outrun her. But stopping to consider it was a beat longer than he had and the window of opportunity slammed shut. "Dougie sleeps in pajamas, not in his underwear. I bought them for him. They have fire trucks on them. He loves fire trucks."

No, he didn't. Douglas didn't give a rip about fire trucks but his mother thought they were cute so she'd bought him fire truck toys and hats and put pictures on the walls. Douglas just rolled his eyes when he told Rusty about it, said—

Douglas was dead.

The reality of that slammed into Rusty's chest like a wrecking ball. He'd been bitten by a rattlesnake and he had died. Rusty had been so sick when he got to the Middle of Nowhere he'd been able to do nothing but vomit, barely aware of his surroundings. But he'd known when Douglas's mother showed up. And he'd been sufficiently recovered when she started screaming that he'd murdered her son to understand what she was saying.

Suddenly, Rusty felt an iron grip of fingers around his upper arm, fingernails digging into his flesh. Mrs. McFarland yanked him up out of the bed and shoved him toward the doorway.

"Come on!"

He stumbled on purpose and went down on one knee

so he could snatch up his jeans off the floor. He got back to his feet with her still holding onto him and danced on one foot while he stuck the other down his pants leg. She let him pull his pants on, but then shoved him toward the door of his room without letting him get a shirt or shoes.

As soon as she let go of him and pushed, he leapt through the doorway … and kept running, dashed down the hall to the kitchen and the back door.

He was a step away from it when the gunshot exploded like a bomb in the small room and a hole appeared in the wall a couple of feet from where he was standing.

"Stop right there or I will put a bullet between your shoulder blades."

Where had she gotten a gun? She hadn't had a gun when … or did she? She only grabbed him with one hand. In her pocket …?

He skidded to a stop in bare feet and turned toward where she stood, leveling a small pistol at him. She held it in a two-hand "cop's grip" but she was doing it wrong, had her fingers in the wrong place. She had one on the trigger, though, and that was all that mattered.

"You're coming with me. Out the door, walk slow to my car."

Rusty'd thought that the sound of that rattlesnake and Douglas's screams was scary. He'd believed at the time that nothing in life would ever be more scary than that. But he'd been wrong. He was so frightened now at the sight of the gun that he came very close to losing control over his bladder and peeing himself.

He put his hands up. She didn't tell him to, but he did. She gestured with the gun barrel and he stepped up to the back door and opened it and then the screen. Her car was parked in his empty driveway with the lid of the trunk standing open.

"Get in the trunk."

He looked at her as if to say, "Seriously?" and knew instantly she was … *dead* serious.

He crossed the yard, angling toward the back of the car across the lawn. He could feel the long grass with his bare feet. He needed to mow it. His mom had been telling him for days—

Then he screamed. Or made some kind of sound, a wail or a grunt … something.

He had drawn even with the car and could see in through the driver's window. Could see what was in the front seat.

It was Douglas. Douglas's dead body.

His mother had strapped him in with the seatbelt.

Chapter Twenty-Nine

Cotton Jackson pulled into the driveway of the house he'd lived in for twenty-five years, furnished now with only the basics of camping equipment and yard sale furniture, the house from which all his belongings, and his precious wife Thelma, had vanished two weeks ago.

The van with the television-show logo for *If You've Got It, Haunt It* was parked on the other side of the driveway in front of the two-car garage.

Cotton had run a couple of errands after his conversation with Rose Topple in the nursing home and had hit a wall of exhaustion, wanted to curl up and go to sleep in the Kroger parking lot after he'd gotten the necessary few groceries, and an assortment of over-the-counter medications to keep the three of them awake.

"I'm too old for this," he moaned to himself as he got behind the wheel, and in truth he felt older than a mere sixty-four years of living would explain. Old and tired. He rolled the windows down to focus cool air into his face and turned the radio up as high as it would go. It was a lost cause, though. Once on the road, he quickly got so drowsy he didn't trust himself to make it all the way back to Nowhere County, was forced to pull over into the parking lot of a Carlisle strip mall to take a quick nap. He didn't think he'd sleep but a few minutes — and would likely wake up screaming, but he was wrong on both counts. He slept soundly for several hours and might have slept even longer if the rumble of thunder hadn't awakened him. To his surprise, he woke up refreshed. And it wasn't hard to figure out why. The oppression he'd felt every minute in Nowhere County had lifted as soon as he crossed into Beaufort County. The tension had drained away like the air out of a balloon and he'd slept soundly until he awakened with a start to a leaden sky boiling with storm clouds. It was the middle of the afternoon.

"We were about to send out the sled dogs and the Royal Canadian Mounted Police," Jolene said when she looked up and saw him in the kitchen doorway.

"Figured the old lady was holding you captive … for what possible reason we couldn't fathom," Stuart said, then seriously, "or you fell asleep at the wheel and ran off the road and down the side of a mountain."

"Close, but no cigar," Cotton said, and fit a smile on his face that hung as limp as a wet sheet on a clothesline. He thought maybe he better keep his mouth shut and not tell Jolene and Stuart anything — the two of them looked awful, somewhere on the other side of exhausted. They looked like they'd aged ten years.

It was clear without even asking that their mission to retrieve Jolene's ghost-busting equipment from Reece Tibbits's house had not gone well.

Cotton's brief respite had refreshed him more than could be explained by a couple hours of sleep. It was more about being able to breathe without feeling like an elephant was sitting on his chest. Jolene and Stuart needed a break like that, too. Jolene could take one, but Stuart couldn't … or he'd forget what he'd come here to do.

"Well?" Jolene said, and the two of them looked at him expectantly. "Do we have to insert a quarter to get the jukebox to start playing a song?"

"I think I have an address: Jabberwock, Fearsome Hollow, Nowhere County, Kentucky."

"That's what she said, the old lady — that the thing that made everybody vanish, lives there?" Stuart asked.

"Rose Topple told me that the town of Gideon and everybody in it vanished overnight. Just like she told Thelma. And I'm convinced it's not some concocted story. It's the truth. The town really did go poof in a puff of smoke. She said the 'Jabberwock' took it."

"Seriously?" Stuart's face lost some of its exhausted look as his interest animated it. "She used that word — called it the same thing Shep Clayton called it?"

Cotton nodded.

"If this Jabberwock thing made Gideon vanish, it made the rest of Nowhere County vanish, too," Jolene said.

"And after the town vanished, the Jabberwock was *still there*. It talked to Lily, told her things."

"What things?" Stuart asked.

"She shut down before we got to that part, but the point is, if it remained in Fearsome Hollow after it gobbled up Gideon, it's a safe bet it's *still* there."

They looked from one to the other and it was clear nobody disagreed.

"So did you guys get the equipment back from Reece's?" Cotton asked. "Meet any interesting people in the process?"

The air seemed to drain out of both of them and they looked as tired and disheartened as they had when he came in.

"I take back the question," Cotton said. "I don't want to have to jam anything else into my head right now. Not another word until we eat." Cotton reached into the sack he'd brought into the house and looked at Jolene. "There's white meat and dark meat, but you are not restricted to eating the meat that corresponds to your ethnicity."

"Is that another white-person joke?"

"I got Colonel Poc-Poc on my way out of Carlisle," Cotton told Stuart.

"Colonel Poc-Poc?"

"What mountain people call Kentucky Fried Chicken. Colonel, as in Colonel Sanders."

"And poc-poc as in the sound a chicken makes." Jolene then did a reasonably good imitation of one. "Poc, poc, poc-poc-pooooc."

Cotton began to empty the contents of the bag onto the table, deflecting all questions until "we got some food in our bellies."

"Cotton's right," Stuart said. "I have something resembling an appetite and I don't think I want to hear the story of Rose Topple and the nursing home on an empty stomach."

They ate like they hadn't had a meal in weeks. By mutual unspoken agreement, conversation was relegated to the relative superiority of original recipe chicken versus extra crispy, a Jolene soliloquy, "ode to a Colonel Sanders biscuit," and general belly-aching about the cardboard nature of KFC fries.

"There's more flavor in a Styrofoam packing worm," Jolene said.

As they cleared away the greasy paper plates, Stuart and Jolene told Cotton that Jolene's equipment was still there and there'd been no reception committee waiting for them at the Tibbits house.

"Well, that's good news!"

"The only good news," Jolene said. "The equipment was there. The readings weren't. Everything we recorded, all the data had been erased."

Cotton recoiled from the words like from a physical blow, only then realizing how much he'd been banking on Jolene spreading the story to the world.

"So we decided to get *new* data — at Charlie's mother's house," Stuart said but hope died in Cotton's chest before it had a chance to draw first breath.

"Nobody home," Jolene said. "Literally. Dead line. Not even a dial tone."

"It was just a house — an *empty* house," Stuart said, his voice ragged.

"No more paranormal activity there than all the 'haunted houses' I visited where I faked the presence of ghosts."

They sat silent for a moment, then Stuart plunged relentlessly forward. Cotton was impressed by his tenacity.

"So spill … was Rose Topple senile?"

"Absolutely not!"

Cotton began his tale, told them the stories Rose Topple had told him. He'd been trying to organize it all in his head into some rational narrative, but had not been able to do much with the tangled tale but repeat it to the two of them as it was told to him. He described how the miner found bones, skeletons in the mine, and how the rest of the miners refused to go back to work, afraid they'd desecrated an Indian burial ground and the mine would be haunted.

"A representative of the mining company showed up and told them the bones were the remains of a village of 'jigger-dancers' that'd been massacred by Indians."

"Jigger dancers?" Stuart asked.

"I think he was talking about Shakers — a sect, some spinoff of Quakers ... who, as we all know, were abolitionists and therefore not that Southern boy's favorite people — so the miners tossed the bones in the woods, and Lily went home to find her little brother playing with her mother's favorite pot. He broke it, she got the blame, and she ran away into the woods and got lost. The next morning when she came home ... the town had vanished."

"So this Jabberwock thing gobbled up Gideon — did she say why?" Jolene asked.

"I don't think she knew." Cotton paused, remembering what she'd said at the end — that the Jabberwock and her mother had talked. "She said her mother did something that kept her on the Jabberwock's Christmas card list, but she wouldn't tell me what."

"So the Jabberwock gobbled up a little mining town, and given there are no other suspects in the crime, we assume that a century later it did the same thing with a whole county," Stuart said.

"Why? What for?" Jolene asked.

"I don't know," Cotton said.

Stuart stood in frustration, went to the window on the kitchen door, pulled back the curtains and looked out at the stormy sky. Then he turned back, his jaw set.

"What difference does it make why? If the Jabberwock in Fearsome Hollow is what made Nowhere County vanish ... then the only way to get the county back is—"

"To go have a come-to-Jesus talk with the Jabberwock?" Cotton said.

"Something like that."

Stuart turned to Jolene.

"That machine, the one stuck behind the others ... the thingamabob that emits high-frequency sound waves, higher than a dog whistle, or something like that. You said it was bug spray for ghosts."

Cotton vaguely recalled the description of some machine they hadn't taken into Pete's house. "Yeah, *bug spray* — gets rid of them."

"That's what you said, didn't you?" Stuart said.

"Well, yes, but—"

"Does it work?" Cotton had asked the same question when he first saw it. He got the same response now as he'd gotten then.

"How would I know? I've never used it on a real ghost." Jolene shrugged. "I've never done anything but fake readings to make it appear there's paranormal activity when there really isn't any, remember."

"But your equipment detected a *real* presence in your father's house — it did, didn't it?"

"Absolutely."

"So is it possible the thingamabob could actually get rid of spirits?"

"Well, it does disrupt electromagnetic energy, so ..." She stopped. "Okay, *theoretically* it should work."

Stuart looked from Jolene to Cotton.

"Anybody else got a better plan in mind, because if you don't, this is all we've got."

They grew quiet.

"I'm in for this, but before we go, I think it's time to call Moses," Jolene said.

"The guy you said talks to ghosts?" Cotton asked.

"What for?" Stuart asked. "You think he can zap ghosts better than your thingamabob?"

"No, not to 'zap' the ghosts. Moses is ... I don't know what to say about him. He's ... the real deal, the only person I ever met who wasn't faking."

"I've never heard of him so his television show must not—" Stuart began.

"Television show! Moses? Oh, no, no, no. Moses isn't trying to … he doesn't use his … *Nobody's* heard of him. He avoids publicity, has run from notoriety for fifty years. Moses is just an old man who … if there's anybody on the planet who *really can* talk to dead people, it's Moses Weiss."

"And you want to call him because …"

"The people who vanished out of Nowhere County, they're not all dead!" There was such force in her words, Cotton jumped. "They're alive … *somewhere.*" She looked from one to the other for confirmation and they nodded. They all believed that. They *had* to believe it. "That little girl, Rose Topple, her father was alive for a few days and then …" She paused, seemed to screw herself up to what she was going to say next. "It's going to take a while, with thousands of people instead of just a couple hundred, but I think the Jabberwock intends to kill everybody in Nowhere County eventually. I don't want to believe that, but I do."

"So do I," Stuart said softly. "And we're running out of time."

"That's the thing — they're not all dead now, but it's only reasonable to assume that *some* of them are. The Jabberwock has killed some people already — the Tibbitses, the Tungate brothers … I'm sure lots of others. Maybe Moses could talk to those dead people."

"But didn't you say that this Moses guy is … that talking to dead people had driven him crazy?" Stuart asked.

"Yes, I did. And yes, Moses is … peculiar. Strange, very strange."

"Half a bubble off plumb?" Cotton offered.

"At least that. I might not be able to reach him. I have

his old number in Nashville but I haven't talked to him in years and he moves around a lot. Still, it's worth a shot."

Jolene went to the phone on the wall in the hallway. Cotton could hear her talking but not what she was saying.

"It's the right number, but he wasn't home so I left a message," Jolene said as she came back into the kitchen. "I told him he could get in touch with me here," she said to Cotton. "Gave him your name, phone number and address, so all I can do is hope he calls back." She shrugged. "But if I came home and heard a message on my answering machine like the one I just left on Moses's …" She didn't finish, just shook her head.

Cotton looked past Stuart out the window at the darkening sky above the hollow. "I don't know about the rest of you, but the only thing I can think of that's scarier than going ghost hunting is going ghost hunting *in the dark*."

"Copy that."

"You want to wait until morning?" Jolene asked.

"And spend another sleepless night on Cotton's lumpy cot dreaming of *my little girl as a rotting corpse*?"

That was a conversation stopper.

Finally, Stuart spoke again.

"You really don't think that ghost-zapping equipment of yours will work, do you?"

"Anything's *possible*. But going out there armed with nothing more than my … *thing-a-ma-bob* … feels like going on a real safari with the toy elephant gun that fooled all the other little kids on the playground."

"But it could be more than a toy, couldn't it?" Cotton hated the desperation he heard in his own voice.

"The only way to find out is to shoot a real elephant with it," Stuart said.

Jolene let out a bleat of laughter. "I keep seeing the image of Elmer Fudd—"

"Pulling the trigger on his shotgun and nothing comes out the end—" Cotton said.

"Except a flag with the word 'Bang!' written on it," Stuart finished. He glanced from one to the other, then turned and opened the kitchen door behind him, mumbling under his breath, "Kill da waaaaaaabit ... kill da waaaaaabit ..."

Chapter Thirty

Viola Tackett sat in the porch swing smelling the honeysuckle that grew on the nearby trellis so thick you couldn't see through it, mingled with the scent of the roses that outlined the porch railing. Hadn't never in all her seven decades of living occurred to Viola what a wonder and joy good smells was. She had spent her whole life smelling the stink of the outhouse in the backyard. Oh, it wasn't nothing awful, overpowering, just part of the nature of the world. She had the boys pour lime in it — had to be careful not to get any on the seat or it'd burn your butt — sawdust and ashes from the fireplace so's it was just the hint of a smell. But it was there in every breath, when you's pulling an apple pie out the oven or even after a rain when the world felt all fresh and scrubbed.

The stink was only something you noticed when it wasn't there no more. When it'd been replaced by good smells, flowers and such. She lit ever one of them little candles in the bathroom every time she went in to do her business, but like she told Malachi, there wasn't no stink to cover up in that shiny clean room where even the toilet was white and sparkling. One of them candles said "mini cannabis flower" on the label but it sure as Jackson didn't smell like smoking weed!

A part of Viola raged at the wonder of living in a beautiful home with everything nice and clean and tidy and good-smelling, and the eye never fell on a single ugly thing no matter where you looked. Raged that she was seventy years old before she ever got to experience it. That all them years, months and weeks and single days stacked up one on top of the other, Viola Tackett had been deprived of the good things life had to offer. She wouldn't let her anger spoil the good of it now, though. No, sir. She was gonna breathe in every good smell, feast her eyes on the beauty of them little knick-knacks sitting around everywhere on tables and shelves, little ceramic birds and painted vases and the like. She was going to suck every speck of joy from the feel of them silk sheets on her skin and the feather mattress under her like she was a'layin' on a cloud.

Viola Tackett had finally arrived and wasn't nothing in the world gonna take the joy away from her now.

It was a shame, though, that Esther wasn't fond of it as Viola'd thought she'd be. Girl hadn't never lived nowhere but in Turkey Neck Hollow out by Killarney and soon's it got dark last night she was ready to go back home. When Viola'd explained to her there wasn't gonna be no going back home, that she and the boys lived here now, Essie melted in a puddle and started to cry. It scared her to be where wasn't nothing familiar. She'd get used to it, Viola supposed, in a couple of days. But Viola'd had to put the girl in bed with her last night, her sniffling and snuffling, making smacking sounds when she sucked her fingers, and then danged if she didn't wet the bed and Viola had to leave the sheets off to air out the mattress. She'd have to get a plastic sheet to put on it if Essie was gonna keep sleeping with her. And one to put on the top of the mattress in Essie's room, too, soon's Viola could get her to go to sleep in there. Essie didn't wet the bed very often and Viola'd never done nothing before but let the mattress dry out when she did. It occurred to Viola to wonder how much pee had soaked into the mattress on Essie's bed in the house on Gizzard Ridge over the years … but she let it go.

This whole place unsettled poor Essie, especially the stairs. She'd gone up a couple of steps here and there in her life, to the courthouse or church sometimes, up on a porch or up into that building in Lexington where that doctor'd tried to do something about her hearing but Essie wouldn't keep the hearing aids in her ears, pulled them out and cried. The log house Essie'd grown up in didn't even have no porch steps, and here there was stairs ever which way. Three floors and an attic and a basement. Front stairs and back ones that lead from the kitchen up to the second and down into the cellar. Just about had to carry Essie up them to get her to go to bed last night and this morning Viola'd finally got irritated and put a pillow-case over her head, like you put blinders on a horse, and led her down.

Essie didn't like nothing about the Nower house. No! Wasn't the Nower house. It was the *Tackett house*. That's what it was and Viola was gonna get somebody to make a sign that said so and put it in the front yard, had already torn down that metal marker that identified it as a National Historic Site and told the story about the Nower family crossing the Cumberland Gap in the 1700s.

Esther sat now on the porch steps of the *Tackett house*, rocking back and forth, singing that song that wasn't no song to soothe herself, the two middle fingers on her right hand stuck in her mouth with that fat tongue so wasn't nothing but garbled sound come out.

Viola breathed deep, sipped on her cup of black coffee and thought about the news Obie had brought her about that preacher's daughter. They'd found her body in the Rolling Fork downstream from the Scott's Ridge overlook and folks was sayin' that she'd jumped, was whispering she might have been in a family way.

She'd gone missing Saturday so that's probably when she done it, when she jumped.

'Cept Viola Tackett wasn't at all convinced she'd jumped.

She turned what she knew over in her mind, examined it.

That girl had been messed up something fierce — that's what Skeeter Burkett, who found her, told Floyd Griswold who told Obie. Wasn't nowhere on her didn't have bruises, an arm and one leg broke, said she didn't even have no face and the back of her skull was pulverized. That was the part Viola was puzzling over. Her head. How'd she manage to smash both her face and the back of her head jumping off that cliff face straight down into the river? She didn't bounce off nothing on the way down, just hit the rocks in the river. It was possible, Viola supposed, but it didn't seem likely. Seemed way more likely that one or the other, her face or the back of her head had already been bashed in fore she went over the edge. Which would mean, of course, that it wasn't no suicide at all.

Wasn't a stretch to believe somebody killed her, 'cause if she was knocked up, might be the father of her baby didn't want no part of it nor her. He'd have a motive to kill her.

So who might the father be?

Viola swung the swing back and forth, listening to the

comforting eeech-eeech of the chain on the S hook in the ceiling. Listening to Esther's tuneless mumble.

Now a big girl like that — you beat her up, she's gonna fight back, right? Ain't just gonna sit there and let you bash in her skull. Maybe she got in a few licks of her own before she died.

That'd have been Saturday night.

And the next day, Howie Witherspoon showed up in the courthouse looking like he'd tangled with a mule. A mule *with fingernails.* He'd killed his wife and if he was banging a teenager, the underage daughter of the *Reverend* Duncan Norman … whew! Do a thing like that and you'd stepped in it for good. When they caught him, they'd have locked him up and throwed the key away.

Yeah, it was Howie done it. Them was fingernail scratches on his cheek. It was Howie, alright.

So what could Viola do with that information? How could she use it?

She considered.

Might be folks needed another object lesson, a show of force from her as was in charge now. Maybe it'd be a good thing to haul Howie's butt into court and show how he killed his wife. Viola'd been smart enough to hold onto that purse. She didn't miss nothing. Shoot, maybe Howie'd got rid of the boy by now, too — which would make him a triple murderer.

If she strung him up, wasn't she saving the poor residents of Nowhere County from falling into the clutches of a *serial killer?*

Indeed she was!

And Howie had, after all, killed the daughter of a minister — that ought to count for extra.

"Neb!" she hollered out and Esther jumped in surprise, pulled her fingers out of her mouth and cried,

"Mommy." Well, it was "muh-muh" but that's what she meant.

"S'okay, sugar. You alright."

She could hear footsteps inside, but they were lighter than Neb's. Likely Zach. He was the littlest. Neb was probably upstairs asleep. Ever one of them boys was lazier than the next.

"You want somethin', Ma?" Zach stepped out on the porch.

"Yeah, I want something. Go rouse them good-for-nuthin' brothers of yours and go out to Howie Witherspoon's house. Get him and bring him back here. Me 'n him's gonna have ourselves a talk."

"Obie said his truck was 'bout out of gas," Zach whined. Obie'd come home earlier driving a shiny black pickup truck but Viola didn't know who he'd stole it from.

"We ain't got to worry about gasoline. Now go on! Git!"

Viola had the gasoline problem solved, but she didn't let on. She'd closed that loop three days after J-Day when she killed Edgar Paltrow.

Big Ed had a worthless piece of bottom land on Owl Creek Road right next to the Drayton County line. He'd been a welder by trade, back when he worked instead of lived off the gubmint dole and he'd got drunk at Viola's whoop-ti-doo last summer and bragged how he didn't never have to buy gasoline ever again. There was a little Jiffy Stop Grocery Store in Drayton County, up on a hillside probably wasn't a hundred yards from the Nowhere County line — sold groceries, cigarettes, beer, lottery tickets, and had propane tanks for exchange next to the big ice machine beside the front door. There was also two gas pumps out front though hadn't but one of them worked in ten years. Big Ed said he'd been called in when the gasoline storage tank buried in the ground under the pumps commenced to leak and the county health environmentalist had got his panties all in a wad because gasoline was seeping along the water table and showing up in folks' wells two or three miles away.

It'd been a big deal, digging that tank out of the ground. The thing held almost thirty thousand gallons. They had to drain it, find the hole, fix it and re-bury the tank. The whole process took all one summer. It was Big Ed done the welding to fix the leak.

What with all the digging — huge piles of dirt and broke-up asphalt and concrete everywhere — didn't nobody notice when Big Ed come back one night and attached a little pipe to the bottom side of the tank and buried a piece of plastic tubing from it that ran into the nearby woods. It took him a couple of months, but he run that tubing all the way to his place and had set himself up his own little gasoline spigot — had good pressure 'cause the Jiffy Shop was up on the side of a hill.

Viola'd figured out the day she set her boys at Food-town to stop folks from hoarding that Big Ed's personal gas station was a goose that'd lay golden eggs from now on. She'd gone out that very day and killed Big Ed herself, didn't even let the boys know. Tricked him into climbing up into the back of her truck before she shot him so's she could haul his body out into the woods and dump it.

Soon's she got around to it, she was gonna get some-body to fix up his little gasoline spigot, attach it to a for-real gasoline pump ... and sit back watching the golden eggs pile up.

That was for later, though. Right now, she needed to talk to Howie Witherspoon.

Chapter Thirty-One

As soon as Rusty was over the worst of his Jabberwock sickness, Sam took him home. She wanted to stay there with him to look after him, but he'd brushed her off, pointed out that she and dozens of other people had ridden the Jabberwock in the past two weeks and not one of them had suffered any permanent ill effects. He'd be fine.

She couldn't argue with that. But the boy had been traumatized today by way more than a simple Jabberwock ride and when she tried to bring that up, he cut her off.

"Can we ... not talk about that, about the rest of it, right now?" His eyes had pleaded, and she got it. You deal with hard stuff when you're ready, and clearly Rusty wasn't ready yet to confront the nightmare of Douglas's death ... and what Claire McFarland had said to him. So Sam settled him on his bed with a stack of comic books and somehow managed not to hover over him. And, oh, how she'd wanted to. She'd have put him in her lap if she could have! No, she wouldn't have done that. She wouldn't dream of crippling Rusty the way Claire McFarland had crippled her little boy.

Now, as the sun sank down behind the mountains, she sat in E.J.'s room while he slept, trying not to think about … about anything at all. Charlie'd returned to the clinic so she, Sam and Malachi could continue their Jabberwock discussion. But then … Douglas Taylor.

How were they ever going to figure anything out if they were constantly dealing with a crisis?

When you're up to your ass in alligators, it's hard to remember that the original objective was to drain the swamp.

True that.

Sam had taken over E.J. duty from Doreen Jaggers when Doreen left to go home to fix dinner for her little girls. Had wanted to sit with E.J. in part because she needed the calm and quiet. Raylynn would be here soon. Malachi was upstairs in E.J.'s apartment, trying to catch a nap since he'd been on night shift last night, and Charlie was … Sam didn't know where. But if she was still here, maybe when Malachi woke up the three of them could put their heads together and …

Yeah, and what?

Sam needed to go to the bathroom, got up slowly from where she was seated in the chair beside E.J.'s bed and walked quietly toward the door.

"Think I'm asleep, do you?" he said.

His voice was airless, a raw whisper. It was a voice without strength, brittle and fragile. The sound of it broke her heart. She plastered a smile back onto her face and turned around.

"How long have you been playing possum?"

"Seems like … for days." His eyes looked as weak as his voice sounded. Watery and sick, the eyes of an old person in a nursing home who'd been there so long they didn't remember anymore what the rest of the world looked and felt like. Tired, resigned eyes. Sick eyes. "What do you know about oxycontin?"

"I know you're addicted to it." She hadn't meant for that to come out as it had, blunt and harsh. She hurried on. "We can deal with addiction later."

"Yeah, that's what all the junkies say."

"E.J., I didn't mean—"

"Kidding, just kidding. I know you've been bumping up the dosage and you haven't heard me complaining, have you? I'm just wondering ..."

She let go of the door handle and went back to sit beside his bed.

"Wondering what?"

"I think it screws with your sense of time, the way a funhouse mirror distorts your image. It's either that or the rabies has jumped the gun and is at this moment taking over—"

"You don't have rabies symptoms." Again, harsh when she hadn't meant to be.

"Okay, no symptoms. But there are times I lie here and you, Malachi, Charlie and Raylynn are like the ponies on a merry-go-round, revolving in and out so fast it's a blur. I catch myself straining to hear calliope music. Other times it takes a year to think a whole thought. Time gets stuck in the mud."

"That's not the oxycontin. I think it's ... the Jabberwock. Time's not right. The weather's not right. The stars aren't right."

"I don't think we're in Kansas anymore, Toto. That it?"

"Yeah, but acknowledging that begs the question, if not Kansas — where?"

"That Oz song the munchkins sang, 'we get up at

twelve and start to work at one. Take an hour for lunch and then at two we're done....' That's what it feels like sometimes. I lie here and time whizzes by."

"It *did* whizz by, but now ..."

Sam fell silent.

"Come on, spit it out."

"Okay ... the first time we all admitted we'd noticed time was screwy was on Saturday morning at the first meeting of the Breakfast Club." When she'd first told E.J. about it, he had claimed the part of the nerd. "I told everybody that Rusty'd used his hourglass as a test and that there was still sixteen minutes of sand left in it when the clock on the wall said an hour'd passed."

"So time really *is* moving too fast."

"It was then, but now ..." Sam didn't know where to go with her thoughts, hadn't mentioned it to the others. But maybe they weren't telling her they'd noticed it, too. "Now, I think time has slowed down. I haven't used the hourglass to check." She looked sheepish. "Mainly because I don't really want to know. But I'd wager that—"

"Now the sand in the hourglass will run out before the clock says an hour has passed," E.J. finished for her.

"Yup. But why? Why too fast and then too slow?"

"Raylynn told me this morning that the stars in the sky were screwy last night, too."

"Yeah, we've all noticed that."

"No, not regular screwy, *new* screwy. I'd noticed the stars weren't right long before I went out to Judd's on Friday. So had Raylynn. But she said that last night the stars — which can't be real stars because they don't blink — were all on one side of the sky. Half the sky had stars, the other half was just black."

Sam hadn't noticed that. But when she and Charlie had ridden home from the courthouse last night, they hadn't been attending to random things like stars in the sky.

All she could do was shake her head in confusion. "Why on earth …?"

"I'm the guy with a fever … so don't listen to me, but …"

He let the thought dangle. Now, it was Sam's turn to tell E.J. to spit it out.

"Okay, what I was thinking is … the fast-time/slow-time issue, the stars. Perhaps there are other things we haven't noticed. Is there still an impenetrable Jabberwock wall across *every* road out of the county? Has anybody actually gone out to check?"

"Well, no. Not that I know of. You think maybe—?"

"I'm just putting it out there, suggesting that it might be the Jabberwock is trying to spin too many plates at once."

"And that means?"

"Perhaps our J-friend is getting overwhelmed." E.J.'s voice was brittle and breathy, but there was a light in his eyes. "A whole county — when all it ever took before was a little town with a couple hundred miners. Snatching people and aging their houses a hundred years. The weather and the stars and the time, that's a lot to keep track of."

He had rolled over on his side as he talked and now he fell back onto the pillow and spoke through gritted teeth. "I think maybe he's … slipping."

As E.J.'d become more engaged in the conversation, he'd gained mental clarity. The effort of trying to put things together was good for his fogged mind, but he had no strength, no stamina. Sam wanted to pursue the point because she thought E.J. just might be onto something, but she let it go because she knew she was tiring him out.

"How about we talk about this later. Rest now. We

wouldn't want your army of antibody soldiers to be too tired to fight off the nasties."

He lay quiet, clearly wanted to continue but just flat-out didn't have the strength. "How's Rusty doing?" he finally asked.

"He's fine."

"Let's try that again. How is Rusty doing?"

Sam slumped back in the chair.

"Physically, his reaction to the Jabberwock ... he's recovering like all the rest of us did. Emotionally ... Claire McFarland. If I'd had a tranquilizer gun yesterday, I'd have shot her with it. Or a taser! Maybe even a .22! Accusing Rusty of killing her baby by pushing him into the Jabber-wock. She might still be screaming if Malachi -- or maybe her husband, I don't know which -- hadn't forced the oxy down her." Sam shook her head. "It's not a sedative! But ..." She thought about the pills she'd given to Duncan Norman for his wife.

What could she do? It was all she had.

"I bet Viola has a whole pharmacy full of illegal joy beans out there in Killarney," E.J. said. "Shame they're not the ones we need."

Right. Rabies vaccine. Rattlesnake antivenom. Those would be the top two. But Pete was getting weaker every day without his chemotherapy. And Grace Tibbits. Sam hadn't seen or heard from her since she and Reece were in the clinic Friday. Now Reece was ... What'd happened to Grace?

E.J. reached over and patted her hand. "You need to go home and get some rest." It was such a light touch, a feather. So fragile.

There was the sound of voices in the hallway and Sam had gotten extraordinarily adept at reading the emotion in voices when she couldn't hear the words. Whoever was speaking was alarmed. Another crisis.

She got up to go to the door, but there was a knock on it and Malachi stepped inside out of the hallway.

"What are you doing here? You're supposed to be upstairs sleeping."

"Lester Peetree came in and woke me up. There's … a problem."

Sam turned to E.J.

"I'll be right ba—"

"You don't have to go outside to discuss bad news. I'm no help, but it's miserable just lying here wondering."

E.J. didn't even know what he didn't know. There'd been no reason to tell him Viola Tackett had commandeered the Nower house and hanged an innocent teenager. Rusty and Douglas had turned up here in the Middle of Nowhere, so E.J.'d been aware of that. But the rest of it, Sam didn't want to worry him.

Malachi took E.J. at his word and told Sam, "Lester noticed the basement door of Bascum's was ajar — and he was sure he'd closed it after they brought in Douglas. So Lester went to check. Somebody'd broken in."

"Broke into Bascum's? What is there to steal at Bascum's?"

Malachi paused for a breath before he continued and in the eternity of that moment, Sam felt the ground shift beneath her, heard the rumble of a coming earthquake.

"What's missing is Douglas Taylor. His body. It's gone."

Chapter Thirty-Two

SHEP'S head snapped up and he heard himself say to Claude, "We got to get out to Gideon."

Shep was only surprised that Abby wanted him to go there, not that she'd spoken the words out his mouth to Claude — 'cause it was Abby done all the decidin' about things now.

Soon's he started thinking about it, Shep realized it'd kinda been that way all along, from the very beginning.

He liked to think about them days when him and Abby was just kids, junior high school — the day his friend Earl slipped him a note in class saying Abby Letcher had a crush on him. Shep could remember it like it was yesterday, feeling the heat flood up his neck and into his face and he was afraid to look up from the words printed on the paper because he just knew Abby was looking at him. That the whole class was looking at him and when they seen his face go all red like that, they'd start laughing.

He was wrong, of course. Abby was just listening to the teacher, wasn't looking at him at all. Earl was, though, looking and grinning, his lip pulled back from his buck teeth, eyes all squinted up. Shep asked Abby once, a long time after that, of course, if she'd put Earl up to it, to telling him that she claimed him. She said no, but he wasn't never sure she wasn't just embarrassed to admit it.

Abby'd been the one said they'd ought to get married, too. He wanted to, they'd talked about it, but it'd been Abby who was the one said the words out loud for the first time. Oh, it wasn't like Abby'd led him around by the nose or nothing like that, but she'd been the driving force in most of what the two of them had done in their lives.

That's why it didn't surprise him when Abby took charge once he'd got where he could hear her voice clearly, sitting there in that old house, wishing he was dead 'cause he couldn't imagine doing life without his Abby. She started out just telling him what she thought he'd ought to do. Wasn't long, though, before she just done it. Like he was a glove that fit perfectly on her hand and when she moved it was his fingers that wiggled.

"Say what?" Claude asked.

Claude had talked Ronnie, Jim Bob and Virgil into a poker game after lunch, while they waited for Abby's cousins to come back with the guns they'd finally agreed to let Shep and Claude borrow. They'd come back half an hour ago, but Claude was winning, likely cheating, and he hadn't wanted to leave in the middle of his streak.

"We need to go *now*," Shep said. "They's on their way now and we need to stop 'em."

"They who and stop them from what?"

"Them folks as is meddling. The away-from-heres. Cotton Jackson and Pete's girl and him as married a white woman."

If you pointed out a thing like that out there in the wide world, folks'd get their panties all in a wad saying you's prejudiced or you's a racist or a bigot. In the mountains, didn't nobody care about such things.

"You looked outside?" Claude asked. "'Pears it's gonna come a gully-washer any minute. Why you want us to go right now?"

"Abby said."

Shep looked at Claude, looked into eyes the same color blue as Abby's. And he was grateful to see the shift there, the quarrelsomeness drain away. Maybe Abby was talking to her brother, speaking in Claude's head, too.

Claude tossed his cards on the table, scooped his winnings off into his hand and started stuffing the bills and coins into his pocket.

"Hey, wait a minute," Jim Bob said. "You can't leave now. You gotta give us a chance to win our money back."

Claude looked at him, then tossed the handful of bills and coins he had in one hand back onto the table.

"This here's rent on them rifles," he said. Then he turned toward Shep. "It ain't gonna be easy to get a shot if it starts pouring."

He was just stating facts, though. Not arguing.

Shep turned toward the door, hoping the windshield wipers worked on the truck he'd borrowed from his brother.

"We'll git 'er done," Shep said. No, Abby said.

SAM MADE Malachi repeat what he had just said. Even though she had heard him clearly, she needed to hear the words a second time to validate the first.

"Douglas Taylor's body is … missing?"

"Yes, ma'am." Lester had stepped into the doorway beside Malachi. He'd removed the Cincinnati Reds baseball cap that covered his shaved head and stood with it in his hands. "I left it in one of the drawers and soon's I walked in, I saw the drawer was pulled back out of the wall. It was empty."

It was horrifying to think that the closed-up funeral home'd had to be transformed into a morgue because the bodies had … just kept piling up.

Willie Cochran had been the first, of course. Abby had been next … what was left of her. Lester'd gone into Persimmon Ridge and returned to the Middle of Nowhere with a body bag. And they had … she and Malachi, the Tungates … they had picked up the pieces.

Willie's sons had buried him. Abby's sisters and brother had claimed her body bag; her brother built a wooden coffin for it and they'd conducted a memorial service and laid Abby to rest in the family's little cemetery.

After that, Mrs. Whittiker. Then Liam. Then Mrs. Whittiker's grandson, Dylan Shaw. And *two* new ones today — Hayley Norman and Douglas Taylor.

Correction, *one* new one. Douglas Taylor's body wasn't there anymore. It was missing. Somebody had—

"Claire." Sam heard the word come out of her mouth before she was aware of speaking it.

Of course. Who else would have broken into Bascum's to take the child's body?

"That's who I was thinking," Lester said. "What I can't figure is why."

"Because the poor woman is crazy with grief, that's why," Sam said.

"What would she do with it? Where would she take it?" Malachi said.

Sam heard Malachi ask the questions, but she didn't process it. Her thoughts had bogged down when a single one of her own words hung on a nail in her head.

Crazy.

Sam shoved past Malachi and Lester in the doorway and started down the hallway to E.J.'s office and the phone. After a couple of steps, she was running. She picked up the receiver, put it to her ear and found that her hands were trembling and she had trouble dialing the number.

The phone rang and rang.

While it did, Malachi, Lester and Raylynn came into the office, were standing in the doorway when Sam's own chirpy voice issued from the receiver.

"Hi, this is Sam Sheridan. Leave me your name, a brief message and your phone number and I'll return your call as soon as I can." Then she heard the clicking and whirring of the answering machine waiting for her to speak.

"Rusty's home in bed, resting. He must not have heard the phone ring."

He'd heard. A ringing telephone always woke him. He was the first one to it when there was an emergency call in the middle of the night.

Sam hung up and called again. And a third time.

Before she could call a fourth time, Malachi was beside her. He pushed the button on the phone, took the receiver out of her hand and replaced it in the cradle.

"We need to go find Rusty," he said.

Chapter Thirty-Three

"It's okay, sweetie pie. It won't be long now. Try to be patient."

Claire McFarland reached out and patted Dougie on the leg reassuringly. He was sound asleep, leaned up against the passenger side door. And that was the good news. She knew she'd be up all night with him, rocking him and singing to him while he whimpered in pain from that snake bite.

Dougie's arm is as big around as a gallon milk jug, sticking straight out from his body, black and purple, his hand bigger than a catcher's mitt with puncture wounds …

Claire yanked the steering wheel and the car pulled back onto the asphalt from the shoulder where it had drifted when the awful image blinded her and she couldn't see the road.

The image was gone now, though, and Dougie was

again asleep against the car door. And there was a shimmering halo of light around him, like she saw when she tiptoed into his room at night to watch him sleep, which she did every night, making sure he was sound asleep because he didn't like it when he woke up and found her standing by his bedside. Just a boy, a little boy being grumpy with his mommy. A perfect little boy. He always was. Perfect. Absolutely perfect.

He was the most beautiful baby she had ever seen. Oh, she knew all mothers thought their infants were beautiful but Dougie really was. Everyone could see it. The people at the window in the hospital nursery there to look at other babies — they always ended up staring at Dougie. They couldn't help gawking at the adorable bundle of chubby infant in the last bassinet on the left. He had a whole head of hair. A full head, she could comb it, black hair that lay like feathers on his forehead with a perfect face beneath it. Why, she'd stand at the nursery window and after a while everybody crowded around her, they always did, all the other parents and family members, elbowing her out of the way so they could catch a glimpse of the perfect baby lying there, his hair brushed to the side, with a smile on his face. Her baby was always smiling, even in his sleep, and his smile planted dimples in his cheeks so deep you could eat pudding out of them.

"Mrs. Taylor ... calm down. There's nothing wrong with your baby. Almost all babies are born with their heads misshapen. It happens when they come down the birth canal, that's why the bones in a baby's skull are not solid yet. In a few months, he'll look perfectly normal. His head won't be pointed, the back of his skull won't be flat anymore. And if his facial features are still smashed in — they won't be, but if they are — you'll need to consult a plastic surgeon."

. . .

THE VOICES of memory were replaced by a gentle buzzing in Claire's head, like a swarm of bees disturbed on its hive, and it seemed to fill her whole head so she had trouble concentrating. The buzzing was sound but the sound had substance, too, like a curtain. It hung in her mind and she couldn't see through it, couldn't see what lay behind it and that was a good thing because she didn't need to see it. It would only upset her to see what was back there in the dark, lurking in the dark, and she needed to stay calm. When she got upset, it upset Dougie.

It had always been like that, from the moment when she held her baby in her arms nursing him, her body nourishing the body of her child, it was at that instant they were bonded together closer than any mother and her son had ever been.

"I'M SORRY, Mrs. Taylor, but you have inverted nipples, making it hard for your baby to latch on and suck. You can keep trying, but clearly your baby is not getting sufficient nourishment. He'll do just fine on formula ..."

BAT WINGS FLUTTERED in her head, beating behind her eyes, and she reached over and tenderly touched the sleeping child leaned against the door. Her baby. Her son. A strong, healthy boy who looked like he belonged on television commercials, advertising athletic shoes or breakfast cereal.

. . .

"The inhaler will open up his airways so he can breathe, but his asthma is severe …"

A born leader, all his teachers said so. A brilliant student, but well-rounded. Not some bookworm who spent all his time studying, Dougie enjoyed sports and music, sang in the choir, played the trumpet in the band.

"… sorry Mrs. Taylor, but he doesn't have the breath support to sing, or play an instrument. And have you thought about tutoring in math and science? We have an after-school program …"

The buzzing in her head kicked up a notch in volume, drowning out the voices, the images, granting her peace in which she could concentrate on what she had to do because everything in her world, everything that mattered — Dougie! — was depending on her. She glanced over at him, encased in a shimmering golden glow. Like an angel. Yes, that was it. Her Dougie was a true angel, a perfect being who depended on his mother to look after him and she would not, would never, let him down.

"Mommy's got this, sugar, so you just sleep on. Mommy's going to make everything all better."

It was so simple, she was surprised she hadn't figured it out sooner. Wished she had because she could have saved Dougie that miserable time at that place, that horrible place, could have saved herself all that worry. Not that she begrudged precious Dougie one second of the time she'd spent upset. Or the time she would have to spend tonight, rocking him, singing to him, giving him baby aspirin crushed up and put in orange juice in his sippy cup. But if she'd realized sooner what she had to do to heal her baby, she'd never have let them take him to that awful place, put her baby in a drawer! She'd have wrapped him up warm in a blanket and grabbed that Sheridan boy, the useless excuse for a human, and hauled him off to make it right.

As soon as she made that monstrous creature give back to Dougie the perfection he'd *stolen*, she would lay down the law. Douglas Taylor would never again be allowed to play with Rusty Sheridan. A kid like that didn't deserve a true, loyal boy like Dougie for a friend.

The sun sparkled off the metal of the sign in the morning sunshine. "Beaufort County 2 miles."

Chapter Thirty-Four

No one spoke as Jolene drove her van along the winding roads through the mountains to Fearsome Hollow. Stuart tried to distract himself by looking out the windows at the vistas and thought as he had when he first arrived, that Nowhere County, Kentucky was one of the most beautiful places he'd ever seen. Well, except for what people had done to deface it.

Poverty spoke its hopelessness differently here than in the ghetto where Stuart had grown up. Not trash on the streets, needles and condoms, prostitutes on every corner and every wall slathered with graffiti.

Here it was something else.

Here, trailer houses clung to the mountainsides like bird daubers' mud nests on a rock face. Clinging precariously there, affixed by satellite-dish stick pins. Yards with no grass, broken toys, rusty swing sets, appliances on the porch, car carcasses in various states of decay, and even the houses that had not been aged by the strange phenomena that had gobbled up the people looked unutterably old and tired.

It rained hard, a white sheet of water, then it stopped. The swollen clouds promised more downpours as they wound through hollows where the mountainsides came down to the road, leaving room enough only for the road, maybe a railroad track and always a creek.

They turned off Pebble Bottom Road onto Byrne Lane, then onto Rooster Run Road and then off that onto a smaller, bumpier thoroughfare Cotton said was Zebulon Road.

"Welcome to Fearsome Hollow," Jolene said. "Come for the mists, stay for the monsters."

They were entering into a crack between two mountains that rose up around the road, and Stuart could see patches of mist ahead clinging to the treetops. Jolene answered the question he didn't ask.

"Only here in Fearsome Hollow. It's the only place in the county there's mist like this."

"Oh, mists hang over the creeks everywhere in the early morning," Cotton said. "But they burn off before ten o'clock. Here, though … there's a mist somewhere in Fearsome Hollow all day long, and not just hanging over the creeks."

Stuart looked apprehensively up into the trees where the mist clung like tatters of spiders' webs.

The clouds hung low over the mountaintops, gray storm clouds not tethered to the trees like the mist. Lightening flashed inside the clouds and the low rumble of thunder accompanied them up the road, reminding Stuart of the slow rattle of drums in a funeral cortege.

He shivered.

Rounding a bend, the ghost town of Gideon leapt out of the shadows around the trees. It could have been a movie set for some old Western, except there was no saloon with doors hanging ajar, squeaking in a prairie wind. The buildings stood like gray gravestones beneath a dreary sky the same color.

"I can't figure out why these buildings are still standing," Jolene said. "Coal camps were built of such shoddy materials the houses sometimes collapsed while there were still people living in them."

"I used to wonder the same thing," Cotton said. "Now …"

"Now what?"

"Now … I think the buildings have been kept upright. I think whatever force is here … it wants this town to stay here. Wants people to see it. And remember."

They pulled the van to a halt near an ancient tree that stood in the center of town, and Stuart got out and gawked at it.

"Now *that* is some serious tree-ege," he said, craning his neck to look up into the canopy of leaves. "I've never seen a California redwood, but this baby's got to be a kissing cousin."

"It's called the Carthage Oak. I'm sure it's the biggest tree in the county – though not in the whole state, I wouldn't think. There's some virgin timber in the Daniel Boone National Forest that could probably give it a run for its money."

Jolene killed the engine and thunder rumbled menacingly around them.

"It was a dark and stormy night …" she said, but even she didn't smile at the reference. "As we were driving I made a decision. I'm not going to crank the EMS meter and the EVP recorders and—"

"Mayonnaise words," Cotton said.

"Okay, the equipment that detects the presence of paranormal activity. I figure that's a given, and I only have so much battery power. I'm going to plug it all into the …"

She stopped herself. "The thingamabob that is supposed to disrupt and disperse that kind of energy."

"The ghost-zapper."

"Riiiiight."

Thunder rumbled again and a couple of fat raindrops splatted down on the windshield.

Stuart looked around. "The thing, the Jabberwock, the spiritual force is in the mist, right? That's what we think, anyway."

"Yeah, so—"

"There's no such thing as mist in the rain, is there? You can't have fog in the middle of a storm, right?"

Jolene shrugged. Cotton didn't appear to have heard the question, was scanning the world all around, his eyes searching and fearful.

"Let's do this and get the hell outta Dodge."

Rusty lay in the dark of the car trunk, trying not to imagine that he was suffocating. He knew it was just his imagination, that he was having trouble breathing because he was scared and who wouldn't be scared when a crazy woman with a gun hauls you out of bed and kidnaps you!

It was kidnapping. That's what she'd done. And he'd seen lots of television shows where people who'd been kidnapped were thrown into the trunk of a car and none of them ever suffocated. A car trunk wasn't airtight, he knew that. If he could just calm down enough to concentrate, he was sure he'd be able to smell the exhaust of the car. Not that car exhaust was a good thing. It was a very bad thing. But the point was that if he could smell the exhaust, it meant the trunk wasn't airtight, so there was air in there and he wasn't going to suffocate.

"Get a grip," he said out loud. Whispered.

It took all his concentration to wrap his will around his panic and keep it from expanding until it filled him completely up. Panic never ended well. Not one time in any story he'd ever heard or movie or television show or real life — not once was it a good thing for the person in danger to panic. Panicked people did stupid things … that got them killed.

His heart ricocheted like a bullet fired into the rocks at the thought of getting killed and he had to grab hold again and yank tight.

He wasn't in danger of getting killed. Mrs. McFarland wasn't going to kill him.

She wasn't, was she? Why would she—?

Stop it.

He had no idea why she had done what she had done, but it made logical sense that if she had wanted Rusty dead she would have shot him as he lay asleep in his bed. She didn't go to all the trouble to stick him in the trunk of the car and drive him somewhere just to kill him when she got there.

She was crazy, that was all. He'd always believed that and this certainly proved he'd been right. The woman was certifiable, needed to be locked up somewhere and probably would be after pulling this stunt. He couldn't imagine what she intended to do with him, but he knew it was futile to try to figure out what a crazy person was going to do.

He couldn't control what she did or didn't do but he *could* control what he did. That's what his mom always said. He had to concentrate on what he could do, what he would do when they got wherever it was they were going.

So what could he do?

Well, for one thing, he could stop being a schmuck and playing by the rules. Be respectful to your elders. That rule probably didn't apply anymore when your elders were crazier than an outhouse rat. Mrs. McFarland was bigger than Rusty, but not much. A little taller, certainly heavier, probably had him by fifty pounds. But he was a strong twelve-year-old boy and she was fat and old and no way could she overpower him if he fought back.

He had to have a plan, though. Suddenly, he felt the car begin to slow.

A plan. A plan!

The element of surprise. That's what he had going for him. That was all the plan he could come up with before the car rolled to a stop and he heard the front door open and close.

Surprise.

Chapter Thirty-Five

COTTON AND STUART stood next to the open sliding door on the passenger side of the van, getting soaked while Jolene fiddled with the equipment. The few splats of raindrops on the roof of the van when they'd stopped had ratcheted into rain. Not a monsoon, but a cold, drenching rain.

Then the rain stopped. Just … stopped. Like a spigot had been turned off.

The two men exchanged a look, putting out their hands like little kids as they looked at the sky, expecting drops to fall that didn't.

A strange, keening cry filled up the sudden silence left by the stilled raindrops. It seemed to come from everywhere and nowhere at the same time. Not one voice, but multiple voices, blended like a choir so the finger-nails-on-a-blackboard sound was magnified.

They all froze, looked around for the source of the sound but saw nothing but the dilapidated gray buildings, slick with rain. And shadows.

Why where there so many shadows? Shadows were

formed when something stood in front of the sun. But there was no sunshine. There was only the diffuse light of the overcast sky, which wasn't nearly bright enough to cast a shadow.

There were shadows around all the buildings, though. Deep, dark black ones. Had they been there before?

Cotton made a sound, something like a cry or a groan and when Stuart looked at him, all he could do was point. At first, Stuart couldn't tell what he was pointing at. He seemed to be gesturing at the treetops in the forest behind the buildings … *where it was raining.* You could see the rain pouring down on the branches, watch them hitch and sway from the impacts of the individual raindrops.

Stuart turned slowly in a circle, could sense that Cotton was doing the same thing.

It was raining in the woods out beyond the town. You could see it. But no rain fell on Gideon.

Not a single drop.

RUSTY LAY STILL, as lifeless as a doll when the trunk lid opened and light flooded into the stuffy space.

"Get up," Mrs. McFarland said.

He lay motionless.

"Go on, get up, get out of there, I said."

He didn't move. Felt her hand on his shoulder, shaking him, and that's what he'd been waiting for. He'd wanted her to be leaning into the trunk, maybe a little off balance, but clearly not pointing a gun at him.

Exploding out of the cramped space like he flew off the starting block at a track meet, he hit her with his shoulder, knocking her backwards.

And then he was running, full out. He didn't recall

climbing out of the trunk, but he must have done it, jumped out as part of the motion of knocking her backwards. He didn't remember that part, only felt the cool of the late afternoon air on his cheeks and the damp earth and grass and rocks beneath his bare feet.

There had been no deciding which way to go, no looking for cover, or a way out. He'd merely acted on instinct fueled by adrenaline and saw trees coming up in front of him, maybe fifty feet ahead.

He didn't hear the sound of the gunshot. Didn't really feel it tear into his back. Just felt a stinging sensation, like a sand flea had bitten him, not even as painful as a wasp.

Then it felt like an invisible hand slapped him on the back and shoved him forward with a mighty wallop. The force of the shove was so great it knocked him off balance, off his feet, and he flew forward, remembered to put his hands out in time not to face-plant in the weeds. The aroma of their broken stems reminded him of the smell of the lawnmower when he opened it up to change the blade.

He felt himself slide forward on his chest, his nostrils full of the vegetation smell and dust and when he finally stopped sliding, he felt dizzy. Like he felt when he crashed his bicycle. He'd fly over the handlebars steeled for how bad it was going to hurt when he hit the ground. Then he'd hit the ground and it wouldn't hurt — for a couple of seconds. And he'd think it wasn't going to hurt at all! That he'd landed on the asphalt or the concrete or whatever and somehow he hadn't even skinned a knee. *Then the pain would hit.* A couple of seconds after he crashed to a stop, he'd feel whatever damage he'd done.

It hit now, like that.

Only worse.

Ten times worse.

A hundred times worse.

It wasn't his skinned palms and knees that shot messages of agony to his brain.

It was his back. *His back was on fire.* Somebody was standing over him with a blowtorch burning the skin of his back.

Then the world began to fade, gray out.

The pain was gobbled up by the darkness.

"JOLENE …"

Stuart hated the fear he heard in his voice, hated the sensation of panic he could feel rising up in his gut, hated the terror crawling on hairy black legs up the back of his throat.

She had been fiddling with the equipment, hadn't looked where they were looking.

She didn't turn to him, just cast an answer over her shoulder. "Just a minute. I almost have it—"

The cry got louder. And it was a cry, a sound like children wailing. Not sobbing, not simple tears — wailing. Bereft. Frightened and alone.

Stuart's eyes darted from one impossible shadow to another.

The rain had picked up out in the woods. But above them …

"Stu …"

That was Cotton, but he didn't have to call his name because Stuart saw it the same time Cotton did. Above them, straight up in the air, raindrops were falling … sideways. Like there was an invisible umbrella spread out over the buildings. It was a force, an invisible something that shunted the water away.

No, not invisible. You could see it.

It was a canopy of *mist*.

Chapter Thirty-Six

RUSTY MUST BE STANDING TOO close to the campfire. He
can feel the heat of it on his back, like his shirt is about to
catch on fire.

"Get up!"

Something jabbed into his shoulder and he heard the
words through the fog of burning on his back.

He had to get away from the fire.

Looking out through a forest of eyelashes, he could see
only dirt and weeds and a shoe, someone's shoe. He
squeezed his eyes tight shut again.

The foot kicked him hard in the shoulder, and he
opened his eyes all the way this time.

"I told you to get up!"

At that moment, the fire in his back morphed in a
heartbeat from burning to blazing pain. Every inch of his
back from his shoulders to below his waist was an agony so
profound he couldn't seem to breathe around it.

"Want me to shoot you again? I said get up."

Shoot you again.

Shoot.

He'd been shot.

Mrs. McFarland … she shot him. Not with the pistol. What she had in her hands now was a double-barreled shotgun.

She'd shot him in the back with a shotgun.

And the buckshot had peeled his skin off from his shoulders to his hips.

He cried out, couldn't help it, and she used the toe of her shoe to push him up off his belly.

"I'm gonna count to three. If you don't get up by the time I get to three, I'm gonna shoot you in the leg." She paused. "And at this range, the shot will likely rip it off at the knee."

"No, please." His voice sounded high and reedy, like a girl's. "I'll get up. I'll get up. Just don't …" Then he tried to move and cried out in agony.

"Awww, did it hurt its baby self?" She mocked him in baby talk. "Fall down and go boom? Skin his widdle knee?"

Then the baby-talk whine vanished.

"You ain't hurt bad as you hurt my Dougie. No sir, not by a long shot. But you're gonna give it back. Now get up or lose your leg." She paused for a beat. "One …"

Rusty shoved himself up onto his elbows and the raging pain in his back made him nauseous.

"Two …"

He pushed up onto his hands, pulled his knees under him and swayed for a second on all fours. Then he tried to push himself upright, but his balance was off and he staggered and fell again. He heard her rack a shell into the shotgun and found the strength to try again. He pushed himself up, stood there swaying.

She used the barrel to gesture.

"This way."

She backed out of his way and Rusty staggered off in the direction she'd pointed, back toward the car that was parked on the shoulder of the road. The passenger side door was open. Staggering closer, he saw that there was something lying in the middle of the road in front of the car.

His mind was too foggy to focus, was out of sync with the world so that what he saw remained a meaningless image for a heartbeat before his brain processed it and informed him what it was.

When he understood what was lying on the road … *who* was lying on the road, he stumbled again and let out a little cry that didn't have anything to do with his back where buckshot had skinned him shoulder to waist.

Douglas.

His dead body was lying there. Unnatural. He looked like a horrible distorted mannequin lying discarded beside a store window. He was lying on his back and his arms and legs stuck out stiffly from his body. His right arm was a horror, black and purple, five times its normal size, his hand like a catcher's mitt with fat hot dogs for fingers stuck to the side.

Rusty wouldn't look at his face. Could *not* look at his face.

"This is what you done, but you's about to *undo* it. You's about to set it all right. You gonna give back to my boy the life you *stole from him*."

Rusty had absolutely no idea what she was talking about.

"Now, pick him up!"

Pick him up? If he'd been strong enough to pick Douglas up, he might have tried to carry him out of the woods after the rattlesnake had bitten him. Douglas was too heavy.

"Pick him up and carry him here."

She gestured with the barrel of the rifle and it was only then that Rusty noticed it. The shimmer in the middle of the road. The mirror where he could see Douglas's distorted body He could see himself, too, and Mrs. McFarland with a shotgun trained on him. Could see that his pants were soaked through with the blood that was pouring off his back, and dripping off his butt, making a puddle of red behind his bare feet.

"I'M ALMOST READY," Jolene said. She had never turned around, had not seen the mist overhead or the shadows among the buildings, but she could hear the cry that was getting louder and louder.

"Hurry!"

The shadows began to move.

Like shadows stretching out from under trees as the sun goes down, the shadows that should not have been there in the first place around the buildings began to puddle and grow thicker. They became pools of blackness, inky streams coming toward them.

The mist above got thicker and began to sink down on top of them.

The keening cry got louder.

Jolene stepped away from what she was doing, turned to look at them and saw what they could see and she leapt back and cried out, "It's coming!"

She turned back to what she'd been working on, flipped a switch, and when she did there was a reverberation all around them. Like a gong sounding inside a bell jar, they could feel pressure rebounding off the mist above and the shadows that ...

"We shouldn't be able to hear ... feel ..." she said over her shoulder, obviously confused. She turned some kind of dial. And the instant pressure it caused slammed into them. Cotton and Stuart covered their ears with their hands, staggering.

The pressure ... it was hard to breathe.

Jolene dropped to her knees and clapped her hands over her ears. Cotton stood rigid, his eyes almost bugging out of his head, then he clawed at his throat as if he suddenly didn't have enough air.

"Sound waves ... sealed in ..." Jolene gasped.

Stuart felt wet on his upper lip, swiped his hand across it and saw the blood.

"Shadows!" It was a whisper on a gasp as Cotton sank to his knees, pointing toward the buildings behind Stuart. But Stuart didn't turn because he didn't have to. The shadows were oozing out in a black tide all around them. Then they separated out and became ...

It was like what he used to do to entertain Merrie. He couldn't make very many shadow creatures — a rabbit with two fingers and his index finger and thumb for the face. Hooking his thumbs together and forming his hands into wings for a bird.

These shadows weren't tame rabbits or birds. They rose up off the ground like dogs that'd been crouched and were now rising up off their haunches to pounce. Misshapen horrors, distorted monster creatures with horns and claws and sharp teeth in open maws.

The shadows surrounded them. The mist hung just above their heads. Cotton looked up at it and his face twisted, like he wanted to scream but couldn't. Stuart didn't look up. He didn't want to see what was up there that had stapled the look of abject terror on Cotton's face.

And the wailing. The screeching had reached such a

level that Stuart thought his ears might be bleeding. It felt like the sound would split his head open. The world around him began to dim. He was passing out. He was certain without knowing how it was so that if he ever closed his eyes, he would never open them again.

Chapter Thirty-Seven

CLAUDE HAD PILOTED the ancient Chevy pickup truck belonging to Shep's brother off Gravel Switch Highway and onto Troublesome Creek Road south of Gideon. He drove down half a mile before he turned off onto a logging road. It was definitely the long way to Gideon, winding over the mountain through the trees. But he wanted to get up on the mountainside opposite Buzzard Knob, which would give them an unobstructed view of the buildings and street below.

Shep sat beside Claude, rifle in hand, with the barrel pointed at the floorboard. It was a 30.06 deer rifle. Not the rifle Shep would have picked if he'd had a choice. He'd never had a rifle fine as this one belonging to Abby's cousin. Shep had only fired it the one time him and Doodlebug went out target shooting. Put a sight on that thing and you could drop a buck from two hundred yards away. It woulda been nice to have a sight, but he didn't really need one. Shep intended to get so close he could watch the blood squirt out of their chests.

The rifle Billy Ray had brought to Claude rested on the gun rack behind the seat.

Thunder rumbled and the bald tires on the truck slipped and spun on the wet rock.

"We shoulda stayed on the road," Claude said, fighting the wheel to keep the truck from sliding back down the incline.

The logging road had been there so long that it had become twin creek beds. The water that poured down the mountainside when it rained had flowed down the double ruts of the road for so long it had worn them down to bare rock.

Claude had downshifted into low gear when they'd turned off onto the logging road and now the old engine on the truck strained and groaned, scrabbling up the wet rocks. Yeah, they shoulda stayed on the road. The higher up the mountainside they went, the more treacherous the going became until it was all Claude could do to keep the vehicle moving forward, inching its way.

Then the engine coughed and died. Claude slammed his foot on the brake pedal, shoved it all the way to the floor and yanked the emergency brake handle to keep the truck from sliding backwards. He could restart the engine, it'd likely crank right up, but without any momentum, trying to climb farther was a useless effort. The tires would just spin. They could back real careful-like down the mountainside to Troublesome Creek Road, but they'd already taken too long.

The two men looked at each other. The water splatting down on the windshield was no longer just drops that had shook off the limbs of overhead trees. It had started to rain again.

There was nothing for it but to go the rest of the way on foot. Shep yanked on the door handle a couple of times before the door swung free. Claude reached back to the gun rack across the back window and took down the rifle. Shep had put extra shells into the pockets on his denim jacket. Claude was wearing a hoodie with the hood up and he had emptied the rest of the box into the big pocket on the front of it. Shep didn't expect to need a whole lot of ammunition. Two men with rifles firing from above at three people who weren't armed. Shouldn't take but a couple of shots each to drop them in their tracks.

SAM RACED THROUGH THE HOUSE, crying out Rusty's name, knowing she was being foolish but unable to help it. She stopped in the doorway of his bedroom. His bedspread was wrinkled — she'd left him here with a stack of comic books, made him lie down because she could see that he was still a little woozy from his ride on the Jabberwock.

The bed was made, of course. Rusty always made his bed. He'd heard some guy give a speech once, saying the rock-solid core of self-discipline started with making your bed every morning. Rusty had decided he wanted to be like that. So he made his bed up the moment he got out of it.

"Rusty always makes his bed," she said to Malachi, as if somehow that statement would convey to him the same meaning it did to her. He pointed to the shoes beside the bed.

"Is he barefoot?"

Looking frantically around, she couldn't seem to focus her eyes on any one thing. Malachi crossed the room and put a calming hand on her shoulder.

"One thing at a time. His shoes? Are his shoes here, the ones he usually wears?"

She glanced into the closet and burped out a bleat of

laughter. His Air Jordans were right there where they always were. He hadn't put them on a single time since the last day of school. He'd told her when she bought them for him that he was praying every night that his feet wouldn't get any bigger. And she hadn't had the heart to tell him that the chances of a twelve-year-old's feet not growing at all for the rest of his life were slim indeed. He'd taken such good care of the shoes that they hardly looked used.

His other shoes, his sneakers, lay where he'd tossed them onto the floor when he'd taken them off.

She opened the closet door, checked. He had an ancient pair of high-tops, some hiking boots and a pair of flip-flops. They all were there.

"Yes, he's barefoot."

It hit her then, the realization landed on her chest with both feet. She had been denying it on the whole drive from the Middle of Nowhere. There was some reasonable explanation for why Rusty had failed to answer the phone. He'd gone outside … was …?

He was taking a shower. Possible, not likely. Not voluntarily. And you could hear the phone ring in the shower.

He was …

She'd come up with a basketful of ridiculous reasons for why he hadn't answered, but standing in his bedroom beside his rumpled bed, none of them held any water.

She looked pleadingly into Malachi's eyes — there was such tenderness and compassion there. She should have cared about that, about him looking at her like that. But right now it didn't mean beans.

"It's not really … she couldn't … wouldn't …"

The compassion never wavered, but he refused to coddle her.

"It's obvious Rusty didn't leave here willingly. Somebody forced him to leave without even putting on his shoes. It was Claire, alright."

She sat down hard on the edge of the bed. Collapsed. Couldn't breathe.

"If she'd wanted to harm him, she could have done that here. She took him somewhere. For some reason."

"I can't imagine what …"

She couldn't seem to complete a sentence.

Malachi sat down beside her and actually took her hand.

"Let's figure this out. She took her son's body … his dead body. What for?"

Sam said nothing because she could think of nothing to say. It was insane. Yeah, that's right. It was insane.

"Then she came here and got Rusty. Why would she want them both? What did she plan to do with them?"

Sam had no idea.

Chapter Thirty-Eight

STUART STAGGERED FORWARD, gasping for breath, grabbed Jolene's shoulders and lifted her upright in one mighty yank, shoving her toward the equipment in the back of the van.

"Turn it off!" he cried, shouted in her ear as he shoved her, felt himself falling forward from the momentum, crashing into the back of her as she fell through the open door onto the floor of the van.

Half in, half out of the van, the top part of Stuart's body was pinning Jolene down and Stuart managed to roll over to get his weight off her. Moving to the side placed him on his back next to the big box-like thing that was like some kind of speaker, the ghost-buster thingy. He hadn't the strength to move away from it, but gravity dragged him out of the van when his knees buckled, unable to hold his weight, and he began to slide down to the ground beside the open side door. Beyond the van was only writhing shadows and faces ... faces in the mist above.

The screech in his head was—

The sound stopped. It still rang in his skull in after-shocks, but the screaming and wailing had ceased. He drew in a breath and there was air, enough to give him the strength not to sink all the way to the ground but to catch himself and push his body upward with his knees, staggering to his feet.

It was lighter, brighter. The monsters were not as black, were fading. He reached out his hand to Jolene, she took it and …

Something banged into the door beside him and the glass shattered, raining down on the ground around him.

He heard the sound then, even in the reverberations in his ears, he heard the gunshot.

"Jolene!" he cried.

Jolene was going blind, a circle of blackness all around her was closing like the mouth of a drawstring bag. Then she felt Stuart's hands lift her, shove her toward the open side door of the van. "Turn it off!"

He fell on top of her, then rolled away and she reached out feeling, barely able to see. There was not one single switch that would … She had to flip the … and dial down the … turn the knob.

She couldn't think.

The machine made no sound, at least not one in a decibel range of the human ear. But reverberating out from the van, the sound waves had hit something solid … invisible, but solid, and bounced back. As more and more waves pulsed out, blasted out, the pressure inside the … what? Some kind of *invisible bubble!* … grew greater and greater. Incredible pressure. There should only have been a hum she could feel in the fillings of her teeth as the sound waves pulsed out and away. Instead, the pressure of the confined sound waves was … suffocating.

A random handful of synapses firing somewhere in her brain registered understanding. The Elmer Fudd rifle had fired after all, had hit its mark, had hurt the Jabberwock. Hurt it bad and it had screamed, squealed in agony … and then *fought back*, dropped an invisible bell jar around the van to make them turn it off. No … *it* didn't scream. *They screamed. Plural.*

Fine, okay, I give up, you win. Uncle!

Jolene's searching hands fell on a wire and she yanked, pulled as hard as she could, felt it let go. The little green light on the machine blinked out. The humming vibration stilled.

The iron band that had been around her chest loosened. She could draw in a breath, sucked in a huge gasp of air. Stuart was standing beside the open van door with his hand extended. She shakily reached out to him and he pulled her … and then the window beside her suddenly exploded, pieces of glass flying everywhere.

What in the worl—?

She felt a sudden stab of pain, like she'd been impaled with a skewer and the force of the blow knocked her into Stuart. She heard her name from a long way off. Then the drawstring bag around Jolene's vision pulled shut and the world went black.

~

"Somebody's shooting at us," Cotton cried.

Jolene had lurched toward Stuart and collapsed in his arms, knocking him to the ground beside Cotton, who had been on his knees, but flattened himself on his belly at the sound of the second "bang."

Cotton had no idea what direction the shots were coming from. Suddenly, the rain hit, like driving out into a blinding storm from beneath an overpass. Cotton could see hardly anything in the downpour, but he poked Stuart's leg and pointed.

"This way," he cried and began to belly crawl around the front of the van to the driver's side.

He heard more gunfire and he kept crawling.

When he reached the driver's side door, he looked under the van and could see Stuart still on the ground on the other side of the van in front of the open side door. Though reluctant to stand because he had no idea where the gunfire was coming from, he had to take the chance. In his best old man's imitation of leaping to his feet he yanked open the door and leapt inside.

The sudden absence of rain in his face granted Cotton vision and he looked over the seat to see Stuart leap up and shove Jolene into the van in front of him. Without closing the door, Stuart cried, "Drive!" then threw his body on top of Jolene's.

There was a *thunk, thunk-thunk, thunk* sound on the passenger side of the van.

Cotton turned the key, and started the engine just as the back window blew out. He shoved the transmission into drive, and slammed his foot down on the accelerator and the van leapt forward into the downpour. Jolene had parked beside the big tree stump with the front of the van pointed at the road. Cotton took it on faith there wasn't anything in front of them because he could see nothing in the downpour.

Fumbling for the windshield wipers, they suddenly

came to life, clearing the windshield in time for Cotton to turn the wheel to keep the van from sideswiping the raised walkway of a porch.

With the back of the van fishtailing on the wet dirt, they flew down the road in the rain.

Chapter Thirty-Nine

RUSTY HAD BROKEN his arm playing on a jungle gym when he was in the first grade. It had hurt so bad he had vomited from the pain. He didn't believe anything would ever again hurt as bad as that had hurt. He'd been wrong. This did. A back full of buckshot did.

"I told you to pick him up," Mrs. McFarland said and all he could do was look at her and try not to cry.

"I can't carry him. When we were in the woods, I tried—"

She came at him, lunged at him, and he thought she was going to hit him with the rifle. She probably intended to do just that, but she caught herself before she did.

"Don't you *dare* stand there and lie to me about trying to help my baby. You forced him to go into the woods where it's dangerous. I know my baby. I told him not to go there and he wouldn't have if you hadn't forced him. You had it all planned out, all along."

He could barely speak, the pain so took his breath away.

"What planned …?"

"You wanted to ride the Jabberwock. Thought it would be fun, like all them boys did when it first happened, all them stupid teenagers thought it would be a good time. You's just like 'em. But you was a coward, afraid to do it by yourself. You planned all along to force my Dougie to go with you. Didn't you? *Didn't you?*"

He was afraid of what she would do if he said no, so he said nothing at all.

"But my Dougie wouldn't do it, would he? He knew I wouldn't want him to do a thing like that. He refused. He turned and walked away, didn't he? Stood up to you even though you was bigger and stronger. Wouldn't let you push him around, no sir. And then that little snake bit him." She paused and her eyes grew brighter. "You had that all planned out, too, didn't you? You seen that snake and you shoved him down, tripped him so he landed right on top of it." She was so infuriated at the scene she was painting in her head Rusty was certain she would shoot him down where he stood.

"No … I didn't trip …"

Rusty hurt so bad he couldn't form words.

Her eyes blazed, then the look in them shifted.

"Of course, you didn't. My precious Dougie saw the snake and fell on it on purpose!" Her eyes were clouded with insanity. "He did it to save you. Like a soldier jumps on a hand grenade to save his buddies. My brave boy sacrificed himself for you!"

Her eyes refocused on him, her look razor sharp with rage.

"And what did you do? Were you grateful that he'd saved your life? No! You took advantage of him. He was hurt, too sick to fight you off so you dragged him into the Jabberwock with you and the Jabberwock ki—"

She stopped herself, literally clamped her mouth shut

so she couldn't continue. When she spoke again, she had that funny glazed look in her eye again.

"The Jabberwock made him so sick! But it didn't make you as sick as it did Dougie — did it?"

He said nothing.

"Did it?"

"No ma'am," he managed.

"That's right, it didn't. *You* sucked the life out of Dougie. Not the Jabberwock — *you!* Bigger than he is, stronger than he is, him weakened by saving your life from that snake … and what did you do? You sucked him dry, stole all the energy from his pure soul. *You stole his life.* And now you're going to give it back."

He wanted to ask her what it was she wanted him to give back, but he was afraid to speak now because he could feel his stomach reeling, was afraid if he tried to talk he would just open his mouth and vomit.

She gestured with the barrel of the gun.

"Now, you pick my baby up and you take him with you. You're going back through and this time you're going to give your life to Dougie instead of the other way around. This time, you're the one who's going to be real sick, and my Dougie …"

She looked at the stiff body of her dead son tenderly.

"My Dougie will be well."

She pointed the rifle at Rusty's chest.

"Pick him up."

Rusty leaned over and began to heave. There was nothing left in his stomach to vomit, but the pain-fueled nausea had grabbed hold of his guts and was trying to turn him wrong side out anyway. He tried to stop, wanted to beg her not to shoot him for not obeying her, that he'd do anything if she just wouldn't shoot him again. But all he could do was heave.

The world grayed. He swayed, dizzy, his throat raw from stomach acid and heaving.

Finally the heaving subsided and he stood leaning over with his hands on his knees, tears running down his cheeks, gasping for breath.

"Come over here."

When he looked up, Mrs. McFarland had moved Dougie's body. Now it lay stretched out in front of the shimmer of the Jabberwock in the middle of the road.

"Come. Here. *Now!*"

Rusty staggered forward, unable to stand upright because of the pain in his back, staring at his own shimmering reflection in the Jabberwock in front of him.

Mrs. McFarland put the rifle down on the road and went to her son's body. She put her hands under his arms and stood him up! He was as rigid as a mannequin in a department store window. Rusty's mother had told him that happened after somebody died, that they got stiff.

"Hold him!" she commanded.

Rusty looked at the distorted face of his dead friend and if he'd been able to vomit, he would have started again. He didn't want to touch him.

"I will blow your whole leg off if you don't—"

He reached out and put his arms around the body. It smelled like nothing Rusty had ever smelled before. Though he knew Douglas had never been buried, Rusty was certain that what he smelled was the aroma of a grave.

Rusty stood there swaying, holding Douglas's body.

He felt Mrs. McFarland grab his shoulder and shove, and he and Douglas fell forward. Then the world dissolved into sparkling black light and he could hear the sound of static in his ears.

~

SHEP FIRED AGAIN AND AGAIN, feeling the recoil of the rifle. He'd already pulled off two shots before Claude began to fire beside him. He could barely see the end of his rifle, but out in front was that clear spot where the van was parked and he did his best to hit the people he could see gathered around the open door on the side of it.

And then the clear spot vanished. Like you was standing outside in the rain, looking in a window, and it suddenly started raining inside the house. All at once, there was a solid wall of drenching rain, stretching in front of Shep, and nothing to be seen out there beyond.

He kept firing anyway. Caught sight of the white blob of the van — it was moving. He fired at it repeatedly, but the image was gone in seconds.

"They're gone," Claude said, putting his hand on Shep's shoulder. Meaning he'd ought to quit shooting because there wasn't nothing to shoot at. "We'll get them next time."

And they would get them next time. Shep knew now where he'd ought to lay in wait. He wouldn't come with just Claude next time, neither. He'd get others, round up everybody he could find who'd lost someone in Nowhere County, tell them the only way to get back those they loved was to kill these intruders. They'd do it. Wasn't no doubt in Shep's mind they would.

Them people down there, they'd come back right here to this spot. Shep didn't know how he was so certain of that, but he was. And when they did, him and the others would be waiting for them. They'd set up all around in the vacant buildings, cut the nosey outsiders down in their tracks, soak the ground in their blood.

Then, the Jabberwock would let everybody go.

And Shep would have his Abby back.

Chapter Forty

Sam heard the jangle of her telephone and she leapt up off Rusty's bed and raced into the kitchen to answer it. She caught it before it had a chance to ring a second time.

"What?" she cried.

Charlie's voice was curt. "You need to get back here, Sam. Rusty's here. With Douglas's body."

And Sam knew. She didn't need an explanation of how the two had gotten there. They'd ridden the Jabberwock.

The night that Sam had driven like a crazy woman from the county line to the Middle of Nowhere to get the key to the kiln out of Abby Clayton's pocket, time had telescoped. It did the same thing now. She had been at the county line where Charlie was helping the wounded Malachi into her car, and then she'd pulled into the parking lot of the Dollar Store. And there'd been no passage of time in between.

It was just like that now.

Sam leapt into her car beside Malachi in her driveway and then Malachi was careening the car into the parking lot by the Middle of Nowhere bus shelter and it had all happened between one heartbeat and the next.

There was a crowd gathered.

She must have run from her car to Rusty's side.

She must have shoved everyone out of the way so she could kneel on the asphalt beside his body. She must have done those things, but there was no memory. She was just there, instantly beside him.

Rusty lay on his back, shirtless and barefoot. His face was pale, tissue-paper white so it made his chestnut hair shine red in the failing light of sunset. He was not moving.

For one horror-filled instant — that she would relive a thousand times a day of every day of the rest of her life if — she'd thought he wasn't breathing. She put her ear to his chest. His heart was beating. It was a solid beat, regular rhythm. It was as if the boy were asleep.

Then she spotted the blood oozing out from under him. She lifted him gently a few inches off the pavement and cried out in horror. His whole back was raw, the skin flayed off, with little pellets of ... *buckshot?* Rusty had been shot in the back with a shotgun.

Suddenly, a car came flying into the parking lot and screeched to a halt so close to where she knelt with Rusty that Charlie, Raylynn and Pete had to leap out of its way.

Claire McFarland jumped out of the car, turned and reached back inside and pulled out a shotgun.

"Where's my baby?" she cried.

Sam looked around then, noticed the body lying on the ground a few feet from Rusty. It was the swollen, bloated horror of Douglas Taylor's corpse.

Claire raced forward, let out a little cry, then turned the gun on Sam and nodded toward Rusty.

"You, pick him up and put him in my car."

Sam felt her hands clenching into firsts as she began to

rise.

"You *shot* him! You shot Rusty!"

The woman held the gun firm, as if she were unaware Sam had spoken. Then Claire gestured to Charlie and Pete Rutherford, standing side by side behind Sam.

"You two — pick up my baby. Be careful. He's not well yet, but he will be as soon as—"

Sam advanced on Claire, oblivious to the rifle leveled at her chest. There was no clear intent in Sam's mind. Her head was clouded with a red haze of rage.

Claire snapped back the hammers on both barrels of the shotgun.

"Take one more step, and I'll—"

There was a blur of movement then. In a single lightning motion, Malachi leapt forward, knocked the shotgun sideways out of Claire's hands and slammed a fist into the side of her face. She folded up in a heap on the ground.

Sam knelt again beside Rusty. She lifted his eyelids. The pupils were responsive to light. Took his pulse again. Steady. Then she saw it. She would have gasped at the sight if she'd had any air to gasp.

Reaching out with trembling fingers, she touched the single stream of blood dripping out of Rusty's right ear.

Malachi knelt beside her and she grabbed his gaze to keep herself from falling off the edge of the universe.

"We have to get him to a doctor." That was like saying they had to get the boy to the moon. "We have to … *now.* Malachi, he could have *brain damage.*"

She looked around then, felt smothered, as if the Jabberwock had closed in tight around the parking lot.

"We have to get out of here!"

The End

The Series Continues...

The adventures of the residents of Nower County (aka Nowhere), USA, continue in *Blown Away*, Nowhere, USA Book 6.

Get Blown Away today!

A Note from the Author

Thank you for reading *The Witch of Gideon.*

If you enjoyed this book, you please consider writing a review on your favorite bookselling site so other readers might enjoy it too. Just a couple of sentences would mean a lot to me.

Thank you!
Ninie Hammon

About the Author

Ninie Hammon (rhymes with shiny, not skinny) grew up in Muleshoe, Texas, got a BA in English and theatre from Texas Tech University and snagged a job as a newspaper reporter. She didn't know a thing about journalism, but her editor said if she could write he could teach her the rest of it and if she couldn't write the rest of it didn't matter. She hung in there for a 25-year career as a journalist. As soon as she figured out that making up the facts was a whole lot more fun than reporting them, she turned to fiction and never looked back.

Ninie now writes suspense--every flavor except pistachio: psychological suspense, inspirational suspense, suspense thrillers, paranormal suspense, suspense mysteries.

In every book she keeps this promise to her Loyal Reader: "I will tell you a story in a distinctive voice you'll always recognize, about people as ordinary as you are--people who have been slammed by something they didn't sign on for, and now they must fight for their lives. Then smack in the middle of their everyday worlds, those people encounter the unexplainable--and it's always the game-changer."

Also By Ninie Hammon

Cornbread Mafia

Fire In The Hole

Blown' Up A Storm

Ridin' For A Fall

Nowhere, USA

The Jabberwock

Mad Dog

Trapped

The Hanging Judge

The Witch of Gideon

Blown Away

Nowhere People

Through The Canvas Series

Black Water

Red Web

Gold Promise

Blue Tears

The Taken Saga

The Taken

The Changed

The Hidden

The Saved

The Unexplainable Collection

Five Days in May

Black Sunshine

The Based on True Stories Collection

Home Grown

Sudan

When Butterflies Cry

The Knowing Series

The Knowing

The Deceiving

The Reckoning

The Fault

Stand-alone Psychological Thrillers

The Memory Closet

The Last Safe Place